The 1891 Muskegon Fire

12/19/15

RC Robotham

ISBN: 149523908X
ISBN-13: 9781495239083
Library of Congress Control Number: 2014901143
CreateSpace Independent Publishing Platform
North Charleston, South Carolina

Dedication

Dedicated to Tom Carlson, who is to blame for this whole thing. I thank him for inspiring me to write and for sparking my interest in Muskegon History.

Prologue

In May of 2000, my realtor friend, Jack, called me. "I have another job for you. Go to one hundred eleven Pine Street, change the locks, and…well, you know the routine. Get the bill for the lock change and the bid for the cleanout back to me ASAP. We have to move fast, for the city is pushing to tear that house down. Do you know where it is?"

"Of course," I answered sarcastically, for Jack knew the house was near my office. "I know exactly; I'd love to redo that one myself."

"Well, you may get your chance. But get on this right away. Bye." He cut the conversation off in his usual semi rude, all-business tone. Sometimes I liked that about him; sometimes I just wanted to slap him.

The house was in bad shape. It sat in a "changing neighborhood," as the older, more downtown areas are generally called. It showed most of the same signs of many homes in this area: obvious neglect, probable abuse by a previous owner or more likely, careless renters. Since it had been empty for a while, trash had built up around the place. Last year's leaves were still evident in a few half-filled leaf bags. There were a couple of twenty20-ounce Old Milwaukee's in the bushes, and a pile of broken glass littered the driveway.

But still the majestic old house stood strong. In spite of all its minuses, it had a charm that had caught my eye for years. Three things came to mind as I thought about this house. First, someone definitely should restore it. It would be a tragedy if the city were allowed to tear it down. Second, I wanted to find out more about the two leaded-glass windows on the upper floors that indicated the house's former splendor. Finally, it seemed that the house contained a certain presence. When I first opened the front door, I felt a rush of something pass me, like a giant exhalation. It gave me pause and got my full attention immediately.

Almost exactly a year later, I found myself again in that wonderful house. It had been moved to a more desirable downtown location and was carefully being restored. I had been watching the whole process from a distance but lusted for a closer look.

I knew the new owner, Meg, although not well. However, I was pleased by a chance meeting when we were both buying supplies at a local lumberyard. It was a normal meeting place for contractors in any town. I reintroduced myself and asked how her job was going. I sensed she felt excited but was not sure what she'd gotten herself into. As we talked about her project, I gave away my more-than-casual interest in her house. That was when she came out with the exact words I wanted to hear: "Please stop by when you see my truck there. I'd love to share what we are doing to our old friend."

I promised I would follow up on the offer. A couple of days later, I gladly visited, and that was all it took. I was hooked.

Chapter 1

Year 2000

"This is what originally attracted me to the house," I said excitedly to Meg. We stopped and admired the entry of her once-grand, now just old home.

"Just look at the woodwork. I love the oak paneling all around. The sitting bench is classic, and what a useful place to take off your riding boots as you come home from being out and about."

"Oh, you think someone owned this house when the only transportation was horse and buggy?" Meg quizzed me. "You seem to have quite an imagination about what went on in this house."

"I love houses, and I love history. Here both come together. For example, I can imagine a family welcoming their guests in this entry. They too would appreciate it like we do and admire the lovely woodwork. I especially love that staircase—the way it's hidden by that short wall with the bench on it. It looks like a backward Z, going first left, then right. The short fluted column with the leafy cap on top of that same wall sets it off beautifully. I love the craftsmanship and wish I had an ounce of that talent."

"Yes, we certainly agree on that. You'll love to see some of the other things I've discovered. For example, look at this closet."

"Very common for a closet to be here in the entry for the visitors' coats and wraps," I said, thinking out loud.

"No, that's not the point. Look—there are two doors in the closet. Why would this craftsman builder want two doors? Do you think this is the original design?"

My mind did not need an excuse to go off on a story filled with possibilities, but I refrained for now. I could dream and ooh and aah about this place ad nauseam. Meg was in love with the house, just like I was. She demonstrated it by the interest and care she took with the details of the restoration.

"I'm so glad you invited me up to see how your work is going."

I was excited to be inside the house again. I had not been in it since I had changed the locks a year earlier. I had been curious about how her job was progressing since I passed the house nearly every day in my travels. I had watched each step: the hole in the ground, the moving of the house, the basement improperly built, the misaligned sewer hookup, and the delay that had caused. I was excited to see the house moved onto the new basement foundation, closed up, a new front porch built, and an addition planned for the rear of the house. I particularly approved of the color scheme Meg had chosen. She had a knack for historical accuracy that I admired. However, I couldn't help but remember the first time I saw the place.

A year earlier, this house had been ugly by anybody's standards when you viewed it from the outside. It sat on a nondescript street, in a somewhat sad part of town. It sat on the edge of a downtown area, now defunct, and the adjacent housing showed significant neglect. The peeling paint and the rotted, sagging porch were obvious. The years of neglect had taken a heavy toll. For the age of the house, few indications remained of any Victorian grandeur or Lumber Era aristocracy.

The building inspector and the realtor who had sent me there laughed and were astounded that I could see any redeeming value in the old place. But there had been some clues.

First, the house was older than those around it. That indicated to me that it had been built there as an original. The houses nearby were of different architecture. This house stood out for me. I had walked around and could see the remains of a foundation at the far back of the lot that indicated a possible barn-like structure or carriage house.

Second, the house had some structural amenities that did not exist in any of the houses close by. I am always struck by windows. Many of the windows in this house had that old, wavy glass that seldom survives when an area declines and windows are targets. The front window structure was a bay curve that was incorporated in the design of the whole front of the house, both the first and second floors. It was not a true bay window, but the front wall was built out in a kind of squared-off curve. It was the front window of the home and consisted of three windows actually, two on each side and a large one jutting out in the middle. These living room windows must have offered a wonderful view of the grand porch or the comings and goings on busy Pine Street.

This baylike structure continued up to the second story, as I said. In the front of the second story was an elegant five-foot-long, rectangular leaded-glass window was set higher than the rest, like a sentry keeping watch. As below, long, narrow double-hung windows were on each side. It was a magnificent window. I was amazed it had survived the vacancy of the building and the oft-accompanying vandalism.

And finally, oddly, there was another leaded glass window but in such a peculiar place. High on the left side, on the third level was a small dormer. I was intrigued there was a third level to the house but more intrigued as to why the only window there would be a sad, warped, leaded window. I'm sure the third level was certainly not large enough to be a ballroom, as found in the grander Lumber Era homes a few blocks away. All this seemed odd and worthy of more investigation.

So my curiosity had been piqued nearly a year earlier. But now I was actually in the house, and my mind returned to the present and the hostess's curious question about why there might be two entrances to a coat closet.

~

Chapter 2

Year 1891

The dog gave a quick bark at the same time as Priscilla heard the bell ring at the front door. She hurried to lay aside the dirty dishes she carried. However, before she could respond, she heard the door open.

"Come in quickly!" Mr. Wallace said. "Hurry! Come this way. Relax. Would you like a smoke? No one will ever have to know."

That was all she heard as the door from Mr. Wallace's private office to the dining area was quietly pulled shut. Muffled sounds could be heard, and the familiar whiff of cigar smoke wafted in the air as Mr. Wallace and his guest settled down.

Priscilla continued her normal work of clearing the dinner meal. She had the water heated on the large wood cookstove on the rear wall. She piled dishes near the sink. Better heat some more water, Priscilla thought, pumping up and down on the small handle, drawing a pitcher of water from the cistern below. The cistern would certainly be freshened and filled tonight with this steady downpour. She shivered slightly as the chill and dampness of the night caught her momentarily. She poured the water into the ever-present iron pot on the wood stove, opened the fire door, and stirred the coals.

"I better put in a couple more sticks," she said to no one. Reaching around the door casing to the woodbox, she retrieved the last of the small pieces. "I must have Phillip cut some more to be ready for breakfast. Where is he anyway?"

As she looked out, she expected Phillip to be caring for the visitor's horse or rig, but the stable building seemed still. It struck her as odd, but the thought vanished as she returned to the task of cleaning up the dinner dishes and pans.

She busied herself while she waited for the water to heat. She took the bread to the breadbox, which was in an adjacent pantry. The icebox was in there also, where she would place the coffee cream and butter for cooling. As she bent down before the icebox, she heard loud, insistent talking from the study. Mr. Wallace and his visitor were both talking passionately about something. Mr. Wallace emphasized a point and pounded his fist on his desk. The walls were rather thin, and the two rooms shared a common wall. She could make out only two voices, so there must have been but one visitor. As she opened the icebox, the door swung quickly and banged the cupboard beside it. The conversation from the adjacent room suddenly went silent. She heard the study door open and then close quietly. Conversation resumed but at a barely audible mumble.

Priscilla found it curious that Mr. Wallace was so quick to answer the door. The ring of the hand-turned bell in the middle of the door was loud and could be heard throughout the entire house. Mr. Wallace had lectured her on numerous occasions about her responsibilities.

"One of your greatest responsibilities is to be hospitable to the guests. No matter what you are doing, drop it, and answer the bell promptly," he'd instructed her, wagging his arthritically crooked finger at her. "It's your job, but you are so slow!" He would turn away muttering and go on his way.

That was what made tonight so strange. She had nearly dropped her armful of dinner plates as she turned to the door when the bell so clearly rang.

Priscilla was very careful with the good china since Mrs. Wallace had also urged her to be gentle when handling the dishes. "Do you know where those came from?" the missus would ask when Priscilla would clunk the dishes together noisily. Then, without waiting for an answer, Mrs. Wallace would go on to tell Priscilla the story of where a certain piece of china was purchased, or for what special occasion, or from whom it had been received as a gift. Sometimes she would go on to describe in detail some place she and Mr. Wallace had visited. Oh, how Priscilla dreamed of that kind of exciting travel someday.

Priscilla remembered one story Mrs. Wallace told about a set of four teacups. When Mrs. Wallace noticed Priscilla examining them carefully, she told her the story of the cups. Years earlier, Mrs. Wallace had accompanied her husband on a business trip to Toronto. They had traveled by deluxe train coach, apparently owned by a large, important company. Mrs. Wallace commented that she never did know the company name, for she paid very little attention to her husband's business. They were accompanied by the company president, Mr. Johansson, and his wife.

The two men were some kind of business partners, but Mrs. Wallace never cared to know any details. She had shared with Priscilla that she had been looking forward to shopping in Toronto and attending a theater show there.

When the visit to Toronto ended, the two couples returned to Chicago by the same train coach. The coach had its own private porter, who served them tea one evening. Mrs. Wallace made a comment on the beauty of the teacups to Mrs. Johansson. Mrs. Johansson shared that the set had come from England, displaying the impressive Royal-Doulton seal on the bottom of each piece. Mr. Johansson interrupted their conversation to make an announcement.

He addressed his wife, though he was actually speaking to everyone. "My dear, I propose we make these cups a gift to the gracious Mrs. Wallace. Her husband and I have had an especially successful business venture. We will call it a gift to seal our business partnership."

With that, the group toasted with their cups, and the gift came home with the Wallaces. It seemed like such a romantic story to Priscilla and revealed a tender side of Mrs. Wallace's character.

Mrs. Wallace was basically a shy person. Priscilla always liked her for the twinkle in her eye. She was quiet, not showy or boastful, but very proud. She would compliment Priscilla occasionally; her husband never did. That was her way. Priscilla respected them both for different reasons. Still, tonight she was shocked when Mr. Wallace jumped to answer the door. It seemed so out of character. He was more the type who would make a guest wait just to demonstrate his power over him. Priscilla mulled all this in her mind as she continued her cleanup duties. The water was hot, and drawing some off, she poured it over the dishes in the sink.

Mrs. Wallace kept a beautiful house. After meals, the Wallaces would often gather in the front room, sitting in the two high-backed Victorian chairs that faced the corner fireplace. Mrs. Wallace's chair rocked, but Mr. Wallace's was stationary, representing their different personalities. She was lighter of temperament, often humming as she went about her daily routine. She would talk to Priscilla, often requesting certain dishes be prepared or informing her of special plans for when they entertained or were asked out to friends' homes. Meals and schedules were always being arranged and rearranged.

Mr. Wallace was more distant, even gruff. The only tenderness Priscilla had ever witnessed was his seeming affection for the dog, Wally. He would occasionally ask her to separate out some meat scraps from the evening meal. She once watched as he took them to Wally, who wagged and wagged, delightfully accepting Mr. Wallace's attention. They appeared to be good friends. She thought there must be a soft spot in his heart if he could enjoy the dog.

More usual was Mr. Wallace's growling and his secretive behavior. Both he and his wife must have known this visitor was coming, for Mrs. Wallace dismissed herself soon after the meal and went upstairs to her room instead of to the fireplace rocker. Mrs. Wallace had a small desk upstairs and a reading chair at the corner window looking out onto Pine Street. The desk sat under the high leaded glass window. Mrs. Wallace loved this room because, year round, it caught the morning sun. Morning sun was her lifeline, as grayness was like a blanket smothering her spirit. Michigan had a good share of both, but winter gray was starting to threaten her moods. She dreaded the gray; the cold and snow could be coped with, but gray seemed to creep in and depress her easily.

"Oh, well," Mrs. Wallace had shared with Priscilla in a recent conversation, "maybe with the pine trees and lumber running out, we'll move soon, hopefully to Minneapolis or Chicago. At least there are more people and more distractions to keep one's mind off the grayness of northern winters." She looked sad and sighed audibly.

Priscilla was lost in her own thoughts. *It sure is raining out there. It's such a strange time of night for a walking visitor. And where is Phillip? I need more wood.* Suddenly, the rear door opened, and as if he had heard her request, Phillip was there with an armful of wood for the stove.

"About time," Priscilla chided. "Is it dry?"

"Oh, yes," he said, smiling. "I anticipated the rain and filled the space under the porch to keep a dry supply ready and waiting for your highness's request." Then he bowed with a sarcastic air. Priscilla would have liked to throw something at him, but with her luck, she would have broken one of Mrs. Wallace's cups or made a noise and upset Mr. Wallace and his guest.

"Are there any leftovers from dinner?" Phillip questioned, snooping around.

"Yes, in the pantry. Help yourself."

Phillip was young, a teen, bright, tall, and a bit gangly. He had a gorgeous smile, which Priscilla knew would one day drive the ladies wild.

"Where is everyone?" Phillip mumbled through a bite of pie.

"Mrs. Wallace is upstairs, and Mr. Wallace is in the study with a guest."

"A guest?" Phillip stopped in midchew. Priscilla shushed him with her finger over her mouth.

"Talk quietly," she instructed Phillip.

Phillip said softly, "No one called me to stable a horse or care for a rig." He walked softly to the front window and peered into the darkness. A gas lamp was lit in the front, which did not give much light. Still he could tell there was no mount or buggy tied at the post. "How odd. Mr. Wallace's guest must have walked here tonight."

"In this downpour?" Priscilla asked.

"I guess so. It must be an important meeting."

Just then Mr. Wallace opened his study door and called for Priscilla.

"Yes, sir," she responded as she wiped her hands and went to the dining room.

"Get Phillip immediately."

"He's right here, sir."

Phillip appeared in the kitchen doorway.

"Phillip, hook up my buggy straightaway!" Mr. Wallace ordered.

"Yes, sir," he replied. Then, handing Priscilla his half-finished glass of milk and hurriedly grabbing his hat, he rushed out. She nearly missed the glass and bobbled it. As she did, some of the milk spilled.

"Clean that up," Mr. Wallace bellowed, seeming overly concerned about a little spill.

"Yes, sir. Right away, sir," Priscilla muttered as she knelt and mopped the floor with her apron.

"I hope nothing got on the new carpet. Do you have any appreciation for the cost of that rug?"

"Yes, sir, I do," she stammered.

"Calm down," Priscilla heard the hidden voice say. "Come in here. We'll finish our plans before you take me home." She didn't recognize the hidden voice, but then she was so flustered by Mr. Wallace's berating, she was not listening closely.

Priscilla returned to her chores in the kitchen. The food was stored, and the dishes were draining. *I'll quick sweep in the dining room,* she thought out loud.

"Oh, that's OK," she heard. Looking up, she was startled to see Mrs. Wallace in the doorway.

"No, I need to, ma'am," Priscilla insisted.

"It's OK." Mrs. Wallace placed her hand gently on Priscilla's arm, restraining her, keeping her from passing. Mrs. Wallace glanced toward the study. Looking back, she caught Priscilla's eye. They communicated something for a brief moment. Then Mrs. Wallace asked, "What was that outburst all about? I could hear him clear upstairs."

Priscilla explained about Phillip and the milk as Mrs. Wallace entered into the kitchen and sat on the stool near the stove.

"No matter," she said, dismissing Priscilla's worries with a wave of her hand. She had a winsome look as she added, "I do appreciate all you do for us."

Priscilla blushed and muttered a thank-you while knotting her apron in her hands.

"I miss helping you more. I especially love to bake. I think it is just the child in me who likes getting flour all around." Priscilla caught that twinkle in her eye and she loosened up, began to feel calm, and also cracked a smile.

"By the way, that berry pie was excellent," Mrs. Wallace said. "I do hope you will make another soon. Oh, yes, I nearly forgot. I need something to take to the Maffetts tomorrow evening, for we are joining them for dinner."

"I'll do it, ma 'am. I have some more berries waiting in the cool of the basement cistern box. It won't be no trouble at all." It was always cool in the small dugout basement near the cistern, so fruits and vegetables were often stored there. Phillip had made Priscilla a screened box with a secure cover so the occasional rodent would not chew or leave droppings where they were not wanted. Ugh. She disliked the basement and especially the spiders.

"You are so dear. Now don't let the bellowing"—she motioned her head toward the front rooms—"from him bother you."

Just then they heard a door open, some muffled conversation, and the men left the house. Looking out, they saw the carriage pull out from in front of the house. The rear carriage light swayed back and forth as it moved. Phillip was driving, and Priscilla was curious to see him make a U-turn to his left and go back toward Muskegon Lake and downtown. She had assumed the visitor was one of Mr. Wallace's business friends who lived in one of the neighborhoods behind them, maybe near Jefferson or Sanford Streets. But the carriage moved off in the opposite direction, illuminated in the misty gaslight. That direction was near the mills and the nightlife that existed near and around them. Priscilla's thoughts settled momentarily on her friend Alex, who roomed in an establishment just up the hill from the mills. But she did not have time for daydreaming now. Hopefully they could see each other later in the week, when Mrs. Wallace would send her to the market for produce.

Mrs. Wallace touched her arm. "I'm going upstairs now. Would you be a dear and bring up a pot of tea when you have time? Also, how about bringing two cups and sit with me for a spell?"

"Yes, ma'am. Right away, ma'am. I would like that very much."

Priscilla hurried to get her boss, her friend, the tea.

The tea, as well as the conversation, would warm them both on this rainy, damp evening.

Chapter 3

Year 2000

Meg was distracted from our tour by some practical questions from one of her workers. I was attracted to the kitchen area anyway, so I took the chance to snoop around. It felt oddly cramped and small. *Hard to imagine how a family might have used this in older times,* I wondered to myself. There isn't enough room for a wood stove. There just don't seem to be enough cupboards. Something doesn't fit.

Meg spoke up as I was poking around, "Well, do you think the kitchen always looked like this?" As she went to the south side, she added, "I've always loved houses with pantries, but this house has these two small rooms. I just can't see how this could have worked for a family."

“I don’t think it had two parts originally,” I interjected. “I think the use of space was totally different. For example, I think this wall was added later, maybe to bring up plumbing for a washer and dryer. Those hookups are there in the one section now. I believe the pantry, in its larger form, was here on the south side of the kitchen, sharing the wall with the study. This was probably one large room, not two small ones. There would have been lots of shelves, as well as room for an icebox and bins and maybe even barrels to store provisions for the family.”

“That seems to make sense. But look over here. What about this sink?”

“Well,” I answered, “it’s definitely an antique, cast iron with the faucets coming out of the wall. They were quite common for the period, but remember, even antique sinks like this came only after running water was installed. The original sink may have looked similar, porcelain or galvanized, but certainly without faucets.”

“No, I know all that, but look where it is. Do you think it sat here on this interior wall sort of alone? There aren’t many cupboards near it.”

“Today we are hung up on having our sink under an outside window. I suppose it’s because we all want to study the birds while we are scrubbing dishes. I wonder when and how that tradition got started. It wasn't so in the typical turn-of-the century kitchen. The pantry was on the outside wall, and the kitchen was in the middle. The wood stove had to be on the wall where the chimney was, in this case the back wall, leaving this inside wall the only place left for the sink. Besides, the sink would be placed so it was directly over the cistern so the pump would extend straight down into the water source."

"Cistern? There is no cistern here. This house has a full basement."

"But I'll bet it wasn't always that way. Even in the city, rainwater was collected. It was soft water and ideal for baths and washing hair. Come down to the basement and let's have a look."

As is generally the case today, the stairs to the basement were often connected to the rear entrance of the house, allowing entrance at ground level. Then members of the family could go four steps up to the kitchen or go on down into the basement.

In the basement, the rear wall showed the key.

"See this large opening?" I pointed it out to Meg.

"It looks like an old boarded-up basement window to me."

"A possibility, but it is built too low for a window. Notice how it compares to the other windows around the basement. No, this opening was a water sluice used to transport water from the eaves into a tank in the basement, the cistern. Most cisterns were brick affairs, usually round and often with a ledge around them on which produce could be stored."

"Sort of like a cellar some folks talk about. My grandfather had a dugout cellar under their house where he stored produce and fruit. It was always dark and musty, and I remember I didn't like it when I was a child." Meg shuddered and wrinkled up her nose at the memory.

"That is similar to our family farm where there was a cellar dug into the side of the hill near my grandfather's house. I felt the same way, always a little scared to go in there because it was so dark. I found out years later that it was actually the cellar that had been dug out under the original farmhouse that burned. Cellars were sometimes protective places, especially in areas where tornadoes abound."

Meg looked around, confused. "But this is a full basement! I don't understand how that fits in this house." Meg was pushing her hand through her hair and wondering as she looked around for other indications of a cistern.

"Remember, you built this basement. But you did move most of the old brick that made the top two feet of the original structure. Look here at the bricks on this wall. See, the ones near the old opening you thought was a window. They are different from the ones over there to the right. I think this was redone when the cistern was removed and the basement was dug out."

"You mean they dug out the basement after they built the house?"

"Yes, that was often the case," I explained. "I wonder when basements became a standard building feature. There are homes yet today with just small cistern basements, only big enough to get a furnace or a hot water heater into. Another house I'm working on is about half dug out, leaving crawl spaces under the other half of the house. Another house has the basement dug out in the middle of the house, leaving about four-foot ledges around the basement area. The contractors built regular cement block walls, not as the foundation but as retaining walls, and poured cement floors. Other basements still have dirt floors."

"Well, come back up to the kitchen. This is certainly more than I wanted to know about my basement." We climbed the old stair and returned to the kitchen area.

Meg got us thinking about a different corner when she said, "Remember, we were wondering about the size of the kitchen. There was a bathroom in the other end of the kitchen, and I have removed it to expand the size of the kitchen. I want you to look at the pattern I found on the floor."

"Aha, that proves it," I spoke up.

"What?" Meg replied.

"This was the house of a family of means, and they had a maid."

"A maid? How did you come up with that wild idea?"

"I'll bet this pattern on the floor is the base of a stairway, the maid's stairway. It would be the access between the upstairs maid's bedroom and the kitchen to allow meal preparation without going near or disturbing the family."

"But there was another bathroom above here."

"Yes, that would be predictably so because both bathrooms would have been added in later years. Now that you have taken all the plaster off the lathe, look up at this ceiling. Look up through the lathe and notice the short floor joists in this one area."

"Oh, wow, I see what you mean. There must have been a hole up through the floor that was sealed over. You think this was..."

"Yup, the maid's stairway, often called the kitchen stair. That also explains why this space was taken away from the kitchen area. In later years, when an inside bathroom was added to the house, it would be hard to run piping up through the middle of an existing house. Therefore, the bathroom would be put on the back of the house, often in a small addition. Here, however, they used part of the old kitchen for a bathroom downstairs and did the same at the top of the maid's stair for the upstairs bathroom."

"That explains a lot," Meg said. She was thinking, letting this all sink in, when one of the contractors burst into the kitchen.

"Meg, come let me show you what I just uncovered. You were talking of stairways earlier, look out here."

We followed him out the rear door, and he motioned to the exterior rear wall. They were preparing to remove the wall as an addition was going to be built extending the kitchen. The workers had removed a layer of siding to reveal another historical anomaly.

"What is that?" Meg questioned.

"The outline of another stair," the contractor and I chimed in together.

"Yes, but a stairway going where? Would this have been the maid's stair?"

"No, but this opens up a whole new inquiry. Have you noticed an upstairs door going out to nothing?"

"Why, yes. The door at the end of the hall opens out to an extremely small deck or landing of sorts."

I smiled, and my mind began to fly!

"I think we have just found another clue to the original design of this amazing old house," I announced triumphantly.

Chapter 4

Year 1891

As she carefully took the requested tea up to Mrs. Wallace's bedroom, Priscilla was reminded to put tea on the list of items needed on her next trip to the market. The rear stair was narrow and curved as it went up. She recalled how she and the children had always loved to play up and down what they called the kitchen stairs.

What delightful pests we all must have been, she thought. We ran in and out constantly. Disturbing my aunt's work and preparations seemed our delight when we were youngsters.

Priscilla had spent a great deal of time at the house when her Aunt Agnes was the family maid. Priscilla felt she had grown up there, just as the other children had. She loved this house. How excited she was when her ailing aunt had asked the family to hire her. She was young for such an important job, but she knew the house and she knew the family. Mrs. Wallace was pleased too, for she also already thought of Priscilla as one of the family.

After their cup of tea and chat, Priscilla descended, returning to the kitchen. She retrieved the small pad of paper from the cabinet at the bottom of the stairs. Priscilla was very organized about her kitchen. She kept the foodstuffs in the pantry on the other side with the icebox, breadbox, and shelves of dry products. She kept dishes and cooking items on the side near the stairs. On this side, she had the baking dishes in one cupboard and all the cast-iron pots and pans for the stovetop in another. She kept the pad in the small drawer in the wall cupboard by the stair. That cupboard kept the everyday dishes and servers. Every kitchen has to have one junk drawer, but even that drawer was orderly and arranged with pencils, pins, and lacing hooks, as well as an assortment of the usual miscellany.

As was normal for many households, there was a large number of home-canned goods on the higher shelves of the pantry. Mrs. Wallace would often help with the canning and preserving. She and Priscilla canned tomatoes and small potatoes. Fruits, like peaches, pears, and applesauce, were also common favorites. They didn't do pickles because Mr. Wallace didn't care for them. Maybe it was because his face was sour enough without pickles making it more so. Priscilla chuckled to herself at the thought. The family was especially fond of peach and cherry cobbler Priscilla made them often when fruit was in season.

West Michigan was beginning to sprout some fruit orchards in the stump fields, as the logged-over areas were called. Farming the stump fields was arduous work, and unfortunately for many farmers, their efforts went unrewarded. They found the soils were sandy and shallow and often acrid because of the pine trees that grew there. Familiar crops such as corn took many of nutrients from the soil; there was limited humus to help restore and replenish those nutrients.

Glacial till soils presented another battle. They were full of rocks, making plowing frustrating. However, the rock piles growing along each plowed field made raw material for some good old-country craftsman builders. The area was dotted with houses, outbuildings, fences, porches, and chimneys—all made of stone.

Many people came to the Muskegon area in search of land. Many of the lumber barons took advantage of that opportunity selling their parcels cheap after the logs were taken. Many immigrants came to work in the mills and camps. Some were happy to accept land in trade for their labors.

Land was a precious commodity to those who came from land-scarce areas of the Eastern United States or from the already over-crowded cities of Europe. Land seemed in abundance in western Michigan. Just as the mighty white pine forests seemed to be never ending, so also was the land. The land gave people the independence they longed for. They were able to raise their own food and supply their own needs. The only thing they had to do was work hard, and many were willing to do just that.

But in Muskegon, produce had grown scarce as winter waned before hints of spring came through. Priscilla still had a few dried berries, some dried apples, and the pie apples in the cistern storage under the kitchen. She smiled as she remembered going to visit the Sanford farm this past fall. Gertrude Sanford was a good friend of Mrs. Wallace's, and they always had a good visit. Priscilla went along and enjoyed her friend, Abigail, who waited on Mrs. Sanford. But the best part of the day was gathering apples. You see, Mr. Sanford was one of the first in the area to plant a fruit orchard on his land. He and his friend Mr. Peck, who had similar interests, had planted orchards of peaches and apples. Although the city was growing and he had sold some of his farm property to the south of the city, Mr. Sanford still had a small orchard. It gave him great pleasure to share his produce with his many friends.

His last crop had been a good one, and the apples were bountiful and juicy. The autumn time was often sunny, and the air had a crispness to match the apples' crisp taste. Nothing like a fresh apple picked and eaten on the spot. Priscilla smiled as she remembered. Today the stored apples would have to do, even those with shriveling skins. It reminded Priscilla she really needed to sort them and toss some rotted ones to the carriage horse, Star.

The task at hand was to get ready for weekly shopping. Friday was the day Mrs. Wallace always wanted to go downtown. Priscilla began to update her list. *Add tea to the list,* she reminded herself. She checked the lard pail and added lard to the list as well. She remembered Mrs. Wallace had requested to take a pie to the Maffetts. *Let's see, flour we have, salt, all the other staples are fine,* she said to herself.

The next morning, Mrs. Wallace called Priscilla to the table after breakfast and suggested, "Let's review our shopping needs."

"I'll get my list," answered Priscilla. "I added tea to the list as I noticed it was low last evening."

"Good. You are so thoughtful and thorough. Please add yarn and black thread. We'll stop at Mr. Leahy's Mercantile and Millinery shop near the market."

As they attended to the shopping list, heavy footsteps clomped down the main stairs, and then the front door slammed. Both women were startled.

"Mr. Wallace came in late last night," Mrs. Wallace replied. "He didn't say a word to me but went straight to bed. He was slow to rise this morning and refused to come down for breakfast. And now, he hurries out without even a good-bye."

Phillip appeared at the kitchen door. "Has Mr. Wallace left for town yet?"

"Yes, we guess so. Someone just left out the front door. He certainly seemed in a bit of a hurry. Would you be taking him to town in the rig?" Priscilla inquired.

Phillip looked confused, took off his hat, and scratched his head. "Mr. Wallace came in rather late last evening, woke me to care of Star and stow the buggy. I noticed something amiss with the rear buggy wheel. When I mentioned it to him, he snapped and growled, 'There's nothing wrong. Looks fine to me.' Then he turned abruptly and stomped into the house."

The ladies held back a giggle as Phillip's deep-voiced imitation of Mr. Wallace amused them.

Phillip continued. "I looked closer just now, and I wanted to show him the damage." He nervously fingered his hat in his hands. "You mean he just left and walked to the office? The Occidental is a fair hike from here, especially for Mr. Wallace or I mean..." His voice trailed off in his embarrassment at inferring that Mr. Wallace was rather old and a bit stout.

Phillip moved to the front window and parted a curtain. "Now, that's even odder. One of the men from the mill just picked Mr. Wallace up in front with one of the surreys they use to transport mail and supplies from the rail station. They just pulled out and are turning toward downtown."

"How will we get to market if the buggy is broken?" Mrs. Wallace inquired of Phillip.

"It will take you just fine, ma'am. I'll drop you at the market and then go to the livery and have Geordie look at it. You know he is the best, and he'll have it shipshape in plenty of time to bring you wonderful ladies back home." He smiled and did his usual sarcastic bow with a greatly exaggerated sweeping gesture of his hand.

"That will do just fine, Sir Phillip," Mrs. Wallace retorted with a smile. "Be ready to pick us up at the family porch at noon sharp."

"Yes, ma'am." Nodding, Phillip smiled, bowed again, and quickly left out the rear door.

"That boy has such a wonderful sense of humor." Mrs. Wallace rose and gathered her shopping list. She seemed to hesitate and stared at the door where Phillip had just departed. Priscilla noticed wetness of emotion in Mrs. Wallace's eyes.

Priscilla knew Phillip reminded Mrs. Wallace of Edward. Priscilla, too, thought of Edward and his sister, Margaret, often. The three of them had been the best of playmates. She thought of her dear aunt Agnes. Her auntie must have been more of a parent to the Wallace children than their own parents. However, at the time, Mrs. Wallace had been so frightfully sick. Aunt Agnes, who had no children of her own, raised the Wallace twins, as Auntie would say, "Like they were my own."

It was such a frightful time then. So many people fell ill over that dreaded winter of '73. Priscilla remembered her own family's worry when her father fell ill and could not work in the woods. Thankfully, he recovered. However, his lungs could never again take the harsh cold of working outdoors. That is why Priscilla's family relocated into town. Her father found work in one of the mill offices, for he had always been good with numbers.

Aunt Agnes worked hard to care for the whole Wallace family, both sick and well. She had to contend with the twins who came down ill with consumption, Mrs. Wallace's ailing health, an impatient and distant Mr. Wallace, as well as the house needing care. Priscilla paused to wonder how she had managed. Maybe all that work had aged her sooner than her time.

Mr. Wallace insisted the children be sent to the Harrison Hospital, which had been recently built somewhere away from Muskegon. That broke Mrs. Wallace's heart, for she not only couldn't care for her babies, but she also could not resist Mr. Wallace's insistence they be moved. Priscilla wondered if Mrs. Wallace would have been well enough to travel and visit the children. It must have been a very sad time for everyone.

That was the last time Priscilla saw either Edward or Margaret. She could not recall any details for she, too, had been very young. She tried to remember their ages exactly. She thought they were two or maybe three years older than she was.

Priscilla remembered when the news came back about the children's deaths. She recalled there was a lot of crying during her Aunt Agnes' visits. Looking back now, Priscilla was sure her aunt Agnes must have grieved as deeply as Mrs. Wallace. She was positive the two ladies were a great comfort and support to one another.

Priscilla did not visit the Wallace home very often after that. Occasionally her aunt would bring Priscilla to work with her. One time Priscilla remembered having tea with Mrs. Wallace. Mrs. Wallace had commented on how Priscilla reminded her of Margaret. Priscilla believed it helped Mrs. Wallace feel better when she would visit. Now Priscilla was at the Wallace house all the time.

That seems to be so long ago, Priscilla observed silently to herself. Then she thought that maybe their shared experiences were why she and Mrs. Wallace felt that close bond now.

Priscilla broke the uncomfortable silence and said, "I'll clean up here while you go upstairs and ready yourself, ma'am." Priscilla rose and excused herself to the kitchen. Shopping was always a big responsibility, but she loved the excitement of downtown. Her mind wandered as she gathered the things from the dining room table. She hoped Alexander might be around town today. Oh, quit, she mustn't fill her mind with such things, for there was too much to do. But...

You get to work, missy, she scolded herself silently but with a winsome smile of expectation.

Chapter 5

Year 2000

As I moved through the dining area toward the north door, I stopped and asked Meg a question. "What are you planning to do with the porches? You've got to talk to me about this side entrance and also about the front porch."

"Sure, but what's the connection?" Meg asked back.

"Well, first, the small front porch does not fit for me. It doesn't fit the era or the style. Second, the side entrance without a porch does not fit the arrangement of the house on this lot." I continued to look and scratched my head.

"I'd really like to do some changing, but I want to accurately restore this gorgeous house as much as possible. You know the front porch was falling off before we moved it. My hope is to make a grand wraparound porch. What do you think was the original setup?" Meg asked.

"For one thing, this area here was not originally a room at all but part of the side porch. I think the original porch was much grander and more practical. Begin by imaging what is now a room was then open as a porch. Before we can go much further, we need to imagine how this house was originally used when it was a Lumber-Era home. We must imagine people coming and going from here using horses with or without buggies. Two main questions: How would guests arrive? And how did the family come and go? Would they have both used the same door?"

"Whoa! Let me think for a minute!" Meg interrupted and began to pace around, thinking. I could see the wheels churning. "First, there had to be a place for horses, such as a barn or stable, most likely in the rear of the property."

"I agree. That is a good way to start so we can see a sort of traffic pattern as to how guests and family would come and go from the house. If we get that picture clearly in mind, then I think you can figure out how to restore the porch with accuracy.

"Keep in mind that this property was too close to downtown Muskegon to be a large farm with numerous barns or outbuildings. When this town was started, it was very small and not more than three or four blocks away from Muskegon Lake. Your house is sitting about on the outer edge of that area. I think this house must have been built for one of the businessmen of the era.

Meg was listening closely and constructing an image in her own mind as I continued.

"Let me go on. When the lumbering started in earnest, say around 1850 to 1860, several of the businesspeople bought large tracts away from the lake. Several farms are well documented. Two of them would have been the farms of Mr. Peck and Mr. Sanford, who were, as you know, both interested in growing fruit. Their homes were near Hartford Street, and the farms stretched south from there.

"So, picture a stable in the rear of this house," I continued. "There would need to be a stable boy, a rather young man, maybe fifteen to eighteen years old with a meager room, maybe in the loft area of the stable. One of his jobs would have been to care for the animals, to hook up or saddle up horses, and also to bring them to the house when the owners were ready to depart. The stable boy might have been asked to drive the horse and buggy, especially for the ladies. He would have been available to put the rig and horse away when they returned. The stable boy would have taken care of visitors' horses or helped their driver care for them. He might have simply tied the horse and rig to the hitching post in front. If the guests stayed for a longer time, the horses may have been taken to the stable for oats and hay and even a curry down."

Meg spoke up. "Do you think there was an elegant carriage house connected to this home? I've seen some very fancy ones before on other houses around this town."

I paused as Meg was taking in all this information and trying to imagine how it would apply to her house. "When I think of a stable, I would hope it was an elaborate barn like at the Hackley House. This home has its own elegance but is modest compared to the Hackley or Hume homes over on Webster Avenue. Those families had extensive staffs and may have had a family of servants who lived above the stable area. I saw one carriage house in a similar Lumber-Era town that was huge. It had stalls for two or three buggies and a similar number of teams. The upstairs living area in that carriage house was a spacious two-bedroom apartment. But I don't think your stable was quite that large.

"A better comparison might be the house I worked on at the south end of the city that had been built and owned by a doctor. In what was now used as the garage, you could see where the stall had been for the horse and a space for the buggy. Most notable was the loft upstairs that had a hardwood floor and a stovepipe. Far too elaborate to just store hay."

"That must have been where the stable boy stayed!" Meg exclaimed. Her excitement was showing as she made adjustments to her restoration plans.

"Yes, a doctor would surely need someone to help as he came and went at odd hours. Now back to this house. How do you think the guests would have arrived?"

Meg was a great entertainer. I could see her getting into this reconstruction by imagining how the family in her grand house would entertain important guests. "I think they would come in the beautiful front door. Wouldn't you agree?"

"Now you are getting into this, aren't you?" I laughed. "Yes, I think guests would arrive at the front. The rig might be tied there or go out back to the stable while the guests visited."

"Yes, and then they would have been ushered into this wonderful living room with a fire blazing in the fireplace, and—"

"Hold on. Now you're really getting the picture. But come back over here to the side entrance, and think how this might have been used. I imagine the family preparing to go shopping and ordering the stable boy to ready the horse and buggy. And where would they be picked up?"

Meg gave me a puzzled look. "You think it was at this side entrance, don't you?"

"Exactly. This could have been the family entrance. Look here." I motioned to the rather ornate door coming out from the dining room area. "Doesn't this appear to be a bit odd for just going out to this small side room with that little door leading to the outside, down those four narrow steps?"

"So you are saying this room was not the original setup!"

"Almost certainly not!" I replied with great authority, although we were both working our imaginations to reconstruct how it might have been.

"Wow. I am very relieved," Meg said. "I want to build a full wraparound porch from the front around to this side. Now that you've mentioned it, that small side room is more likely what remained of a side porch. That porch could have extended to the front and been connected with the front porch."

"That's true. One thing is for certain; this room was not originally a room but a porch. I believe it was the family entrance door and porch, especially when there were children growing up here. Someone simply closed it in later. As you see, it's on the opposite side from the old existing driveway."

"Driveway?" Meg questioned. "I see what you meant before when you referred to a traffic pattern. I think I get it now. But I've got to catch my breath. That's a lot to absorb. Let me get this straight. You think of this as sort of a circular drive, coming in front off the street, then along the south side to the back stable, then around the north side, maybe stopping at the side porch or continuing back up to the front to pick up guests who are leaving. Is that right?"

"Yes. There could be lots of combinations. Generally, however, guests would come in front and family would come in on the side. An exception could have been when the lady of the house returned from shopping. She would come to the north side door by the kitchen, get out of the buggy, and go inside. Then the maid or other help would carry in the goods, because the food would be stored in the kitchen and pantry. Another exception would be when the couple had gone out alone, with no children. When they arrived home, they would more likely stop at the front entrance, be let out, and enter there while the driver took the rig around to the back. See, that would be a more formal occasion. I think there was always a combination of grandeur and practicality in the design of these older homes."

"What do you think of building the porch with fieldstones?"

"I haven't the slightest idea if that would have been like the original or not. I sort of doubt it. But you do know that there were lots of stones in the glacial till soils that were common in this area. A fieldstone porch would surely fit on a house like this.

Look at the house on Sanford near Southern. That has a fieldstone porch."

"I love the craftsmanship of fieldstone work," Meg commented. "Today the craft is lost, but some masons use very authentic-looking substitute products. Yes, I've been thinking out loud too much. That is enough about these porches. What's next?"

I thought for a moment, and said, "What about the outside stairway the carpenter showed us? Are you ready to go to the upstairs summer porch?"

"What do you mean? There's no porch up there. I know those stairs went up the rear of the house. But why do you think there was a porch?"

"Summer porches were a common feature in many houses of that time. Often there was one on the first floor and another one on the second floor. The first-floor porch was often the summer cooking porch; it was way too hot to have a wood cookstove indoors. However, during the winter, the cookstove was helpful serving for both cooking and heating. It was believed that the kitchen had always been a favorite gathering place, not only as the center of activity but also as the center of warmth."

"The remains of what were stairs up the back show us that there was something on the second floor. The door at the end of the upper hall makes some sense now because it would have led to what you call the summer porch," Meg concluded.

I added, "It could have been built at the same time, but my guess is that the outside staircase was a later feature, possibly giving access to rental rooms upstairs. But that's all beside the point. Picture, if you will, a screened porch on the rear of the house. The lower porch was for the cookstove and maybe eating, similar to our patios or decks today. The upper one was probably for sleeping or simply enjoying the summer evenings."

"How could we know for sure how the porches were used?" Meg asked.

I was challenged and admitted, "We can't tell for sure by what we see here. Our city has no organized files of any historic pictures either."

Meg said, "That's all right. I can imagine it though: A real hot, sultry summer night, too stuffy to sleep in the house. One might sit out on the porch and listen to the crickets and katydids sing. Maybe sit and enjoy a fresh summer rain shower. Or maybe drag out a mattress and sleep under the stars or… would there be a roof over it?"

"I don't know. You can see similar porches around town, like one I noticed the other day off West Southern Avenue. It had two porches, identical top and bottom, which were screened in and roofed. As was often the case, the porches on that house have now been closed in and incorporated into the house. On some of the other houses, however, the porches were simply removed."

"I like this idea. Maybe I'll restore a porch off the rear of the upstairs. I'd like it to be open, under the stars."

"Good for you. But I hope you like mosquitoes."

Chapter 6

Year 1891

Priscilla loved to ride in the Wallace buggy because it was so elegant. This buggy, or carriage, was well-built and quite fancy. It had doors on each side, with a brass lantern mounted at each door. The doors had actual isinglass curtains that could be closed when necessary. The family was especially proud of that feature, for very few buggies in town sported such a special accent.

"Yes, ma'am. We're ready to go." Phillip smiled as they descended the porch to enter the buggy, beaming as Mrs. Wallace complimented him.

"You've worked hard, Phillip. The wood trim just shines from your polishing, and the lanterns are bright and clean. You do well. Mind you, remember how important it is to Mr. Wallace that the lanterns always are kept polished."

"Oh, yes, I do, ma'am."

Her comment did remind him that although the lanterns would not be needed today, Mr. Wallace certainly must have had them lit the night before. When they returned from shopping, he must remember to refill and clean them. The rear one especially needed attention, for it had been quite filthy when Mr. Wallace came in the previous night. *I don't know where he could have been to get it so dirty. I'll make a mental note to get that done,* he silently reminded himself.

When the ladies were properly inside, Phillip gently closed the door and took his place at the reins. Phillip drove them down Pine Street past the neighboring residences. They were nice homes, all needing a little cleanup after the winter. Mr. Jorgenson was out picking up fallen branches and waved as they passed. Looking for the first crocus or daffodil added excitement to any spring excursion in the neighborhood. Priscilla and Mrs. Wallace always marveled at Mr. Mathew Wilson's massive estate on their right as they approached downtown. The Wilson mansion was especially ornate, with turrets and three levels of porches.

Priscilla noticed Mrs. Wallace seemed to get a faraway look in her eye as the moved slowly toward town. Finally, Mrs. Wallace spoke.

"I think I read somewhere that the first flowers of spring were the symbols of life's resilience. I might not have quoted it quite correctly, but that was close." She smiled at Priscilla and continued, "When we have lived in and through the cold grayness of winter, our hearts long for the miracle assurance of spring, the crocuses, the fat buds on the lilacs, the chubby robins. Then we have hope. We are assured again of the beauty of the world around us."

Priscilla was surprised to hear Mrs. Wallace's eloquent, near-poetic burst. "It is so good to see you smile and be in such good cheer today, ma'am."

Mrs. Wallace turned to her and said, "Yes, this time of the year was my favorite with the children." She sighed deeply before going on. "Both of them being taken away in the dreariness of winter gives me a bit of melancholy about this time of year."

Priscilla did not speak. She simply allowed her friend to have her time of grieving and remembering.

As they neared the top of the hill near Muskegon Avenue, they could see several of the large mill boarding houses on the opposite side of the street. They proceeded to turn left onto Muskegon Avenue because Phillip would never take the ladies down the hill toward Mill Town. It was a bawdy area with many liquor establishments and other not-so-pleasant attractions. Phillip turned toward Muskegon Lake and traveled on down Jefferson Street past the variety of shops and offices to the main business district on Western Avenue. Phillip stopped next to the market that was near Mr. Leahy's store.

"I'll leave you ladies here," he commented as he helped them step from the buggy.

"This will be excellent, Phillip." Then Mrs. Wallace directed him, "Be here at two thirty p.m. sharp to pick us up. We'll be ready to return by then."

"Yes, ma'am, I will surely be here on time."

Phillip doffed his hat and bowed politely as he returned to the buggy. Excitedly, the ladies went off about their shopping. Phillip was glad, for he, too, had errands to see to. Sometimes it was so boring to simply sit on the street and wait for the ladies to finish. He quickly turned the rig west. He turned left onto Ninth Street and proceeded to George Scott's Livery Barn at the corner of Ninth and Clay.

George Scott's livery was the most-respected livery in the city. The livery was always a center of activity. It took a lot of horses to operate mills and transport the needed supplies and people to their destinations. This livery had three large barns. One barn was just for housing the many horses the livery owned, probably over one hundred. The second building was for housing the carriages and buggies. There were several wheelwrights and wagonmakers employed to help repair and equip the endless variety of wagons, buggies, or carriages. The third barn was where the boarded horses and rigs were housed. Some of the business owners kept their teams and wagons at the livery, along with some private individuals who could afford the luxury. Phillip's boss, Mr. Wallace, housed his two working teams from the mill at Mr. Scott's livery.

One end of that building also had a large tack room containing every kind of harness or accessory one could imagine. There was something there for everyone to fit out the finest rig or the most modest wagon. The fourth building contained the office and faced Ninth Street. That building also contained the staging area where people came to rent or return horses and/or buggies. There were people coming and going all the time. The office was in the front, so that would be the most likely place to find the owner, Mr. George Scott, but everyone called him Geordie.

"Geordie, anywhere near?" Phillip inquired of the man sitting in a chair leaned back against the front of the livery barn office. The man stared at Phillip without moving and then rocked his chair forward, spit out a stream of tobacco in the dirt, and ambled to the door.

"Geordie, someone to see ya," he hollered through the slightly open door.

Scott Livery Barn, the big sign said that hung slightly crooked from the extended ridge beam, squeaked as the wind swayed it on its hinges. His friend, Geordie, promptly appeared, smiling.

"Phillip, it is so good to see ya, lad. It's been too long. Have you survived the winter well?"

Geordie was a tall Scotsman with a bit of an accent. He loved his work, especially the horses. Everyone respected Geordie for the care he gave his horses. He was always willing to help solve people's problems with their horses or teams. He had a very special favorite horse, a tall, mostly white, dapple-gray mare named Thunder, which everyone admired. They would be seen proudly showing off as they rode around town. They had led the Fourth of July parade the previous year, and everyone loved to see Thunder prance and perform.

"What ya be needin' today, laddie?" Geordie asked, slapping Phillip on the shoulder, nearly knocking him off his feet.

"I've come to have you look at the rear buggy wheel," Phillip replied.

"Aye. Let's take a look."

Phillip tied the horses' tether to the post and followed Geordie to the rear of the buggy. "Here, look at the spokes," Phillip said as he pointed at the damaged piece.

"Ay. I see. Where have you been running with this buggy, son? It must have hit a mean hole or a bad spot in the corduroy,[1] eh?"

"No, sir," exclaimed Phillip. "I noticed this wobble when Mr. Wallace arrived home last night, and I wanted you to take a look at it. Can it be fixed?"

"Of course, lad," Geordie roared and slapped Phillip's shoulder again, nearly dislocating his shoulder blade. "Anything can be fixed for a price.

---

[1] *The area around Muskegon was marshy and wet, with little solid foundation for building roadbeds. Roads around the area were often soft with mud, sand, or sawdust. Some of the roads were solidified with logs or poles laid crossways and sunk into the softness to provide a solid roadbed. These roads were called corduroy roads. They were most always rough and needed fill-dirt between the logs. Sometimes one log would sink deeper than the others, or one would come loose or warp upwards. They the cause of many a broken buggy wheel or a horse's broken leg. People cursed the cord roads, but they were a necessary evil to simply allow one to get around in the slippery soils. This was especially true around the mills. For one thing, mills were built near the lake or the river, so there was a constant problem with mud. Sawdust was plentiful, but soggy sawdust was hardly better than slippery mud. Therefore, the cords were constantly being worked into the roadbeds.*

By the way, lad, you need to eat more and put on some pounds." Geordie laughed his wonderful hardy laugh. He was such a warm, likeable man. Everyone enjoyed his presence, but Phillip vowed to stay clear so as not to get another slap on the back for fear of a shoulder injury.

Geordie got more serious. "What concerns me, Phillip, is how this happened." Geordie reached down and dug some of the gray mud from the inside of the wheel's hub. "See this mud? It comes from only one place I knows of."

"Where's that?" Phillip asked suspiciously.

"That is why it's kind of odd. The only place for this blue-gray marl mud is down along the creek bed behind your Mr. Wallace's mill. Now why was this buggy down in those marl mudflats where all the slab wood and drying stacks are kept?"

"Don't know, but it is his mill. He was probably doing inventory or something," Phillip replied, though still puzzled.

"Maybe true," Geordie thought, and his thoughts trailed off. "But who cares? Let's get this fixed so you can escort your favorite ladies back home." Geordie reached to slap him on the shoulder, but

Phillip quickly reeled out of the way. Then he heard another voice rang out.

“Phillip, is that you I hear?”

“Alexander, how are you?” The two young men shook hands congenially. Then Alex stopped short and stared.

“What you staring at?” Phillip queried.

Alex’s eyes went up and down over the buggy as Geordie and Phillip exchanged quizzical glances. “Oh, nothing I guess. Is this your Mr. Wallace’s buggy, Phillip?”

“Why, yes, and Geordie here’s doing a bit of repair. It seems Mr. Wallace must have hit a pothole or a sprung cord in the road.”

“And picked up some mud in this here wheel hub,” Geordie added as he continued to clean it and add new grease.

“Umm,” said Alex in a long, drawn-out sigh. “Oh, well, just a coincidence, I suppose.”

“What are you muttering about?” inquired Phillip.

"Oh, nothing." Alex's face brightened, and he put his arm on Phillip's sore shoulder. Phillip winced slightly and pulled away. "What's wrong with the shoulder, boy?" Alex asked.

"Oh, nothing." Phillip smiled and motioned his head toward Geordie. "Just too much good old Scottish greeting, that's all." Then all three of them laughed. Geordie continued his work as Phillip and Alex walked off to the shade of a nearby tree.

Alex leaned in close and asked, "Did Priscilla come to town with you today?"

Phillip smiled. "So that's why I'm your latest best friend. Just so you can see Priscilla."

"Oh, you're just too young," he teased. "You'll understand soon enough! So answer me!" He poked the grinning Phillip.

"Of course," he replied. "I dropped them at the market, and they had some other errands. I must pick them up at Leahy's at about two thirty. Hopefully Geordie will be finished with the buggy by then."

"Oh," Alex said thoughtfully.

"By the way, how is it you are skipping out from the mill's payroll office here in the middle of the day? I should tell Mr. Wallace about you playing hooky from work."

Alex pulled down on Phillip's hat. "There is no problem, my brother. I am on official business to pay our livery bill here at Geordie's. Remember, we keep the surreys here, and Geordie boards our two light teams. It is near the end of the month, and we try to pay all bills on time. So see, official business." Alex waved the payment envelope he was carrying.

"Oh, OK, I won't tell on you, but you sure are taking your own sweet time about it."

"Better be getting on." Alex smiled and jostled Phillip's hat again. "Mind that shoulder, you know. Stay away from Geordie." He laughed and walked on up the street toward town.

Phillip pulled up in front of the Leahy's Market a bit early. He got down, tethered the horse, and leaned on the hitching rail. He was daydreaming a bit when he was surprised to hear Alex's voice again.

"May I help you ladies into the buggy?"

"Well, hello, Mr. Alexander!" Mrs. Wallace replied. "What a surprise to see you." She gave Priscilla a knowing glance, one that would go undetected except between two women. "Priscilla and I have been doing some errands."

"Here, allow me to load the bags," Alex said as he leaned to take the packages from Priscilla. Priscilla was blushing furiously, but she smiled and curtseyed slightly. "Phillip, stow these carefully." Alex motioned to the now-attentive Phillip standing beside him. Then, offering his hand to Mrs. Wallace, and opening the carriage door, the ever-charming Alex asked, "May I help you ladies in?"

"Why of course, my dear. It is so good to accidentally run into you today." She purposely emphasized the accidentally in her sentence. "Are you coming over on Sunday, by chance?"

Alex glanced quickly at the blushing yet smiling Priscilla. "Yes, ma'am. I'd love to come by, if it's OK with both of you." He emphasized the both, causing Priscilla to look down.

Mrs. Wallace paused on the step, "Oh, I'm sure it would be just fine, Mr. Alexander." She glanced and winked at Priscilla. "We will see you in the afternoon. Will you plan to stay for tea and cobbler?"

"I would be pleased to do just that, ma'am." He helped Mrs. Wallace into the buggy and offered Priscilla his hand to help her aboard. "I'll see you soon," he whispered. She gave his hand a special squeeze of acknowledgment and closed the door.

Alex stood considering something else as he watched the carriage go off down the street. *What was this fuzzy thought that was puzzling his mind?* He pushed his hands into his pockets and walked toward the Wallace Mill. He stumbled on something that brought him out of his musings. He noticed a cord in the road that had warped up on one end.

This is just too much coincidence. I must talk to Peter.

He decided right then that he would leave a note for Peter that night at the boarding house. All the while, as Alex walked briskly back to work, his mind was putting pieces together.

~

Chapter 7

Year 2000

"Let's go upstairs." Meg motioned and led us through the living room to the front stairs.

"I love this entry."

"You've told me how this impressed you when you first entered the house. I would guess it's the workmanship that makes it seem so impressive."

"Yes. Just look at the intricate carving at the top of this Corinthian column. It is so unusual. I can't imagine me doing work like that. I don't see modern-day examples of that kind of craftsmanship even in today's expensive, high-end houses."

"Here is another example of that same detailed work ," Meg stated as she stopped at the landing.

Looking at the stripped wall of the stairwell, she added, "I've noticed the care and accuracy with which even the lathe was put on the wall. Look how precise. Every slat was placed perfectly, with the slats on an angle cut exactly so, including even the cuts of the tapered ends."

"Hard to believe anyone took the time and patience to cut those so precisely, especially when they were only going to be covered with plaster. I am told the old plasterers would take a section in every long wall and change the angle of the lathe."

"Interesting you mentioned that, for I had noticed it and wondered if there was a reason or if it was just by accident."

"There was definitely a reason. The idea of spacing the lathe was so the plaster would ooze into the cracks, harden, and hold better. The plasterers were also aware that boards sometimes warped, so they would not be laid all in one direction on a given wall. Like here in this stairwell, with this very tall wall. See the section to the right where lathe is at a forty-five-degree angle in this whole section?"

"That would give the plaster a better hold, so to speak, so it would not pop off. It definitely worked. Both my husband and I have worked on older houses where the plaster had dried and loosened from poorly constructed lathe."

"But I bet you find just as many houses where, after one hundred years, the plaster is still as solid as a rock. That is a real testimony to the craftsman. Did you find any horsehair plaster in this house?"

"Horsehair what?"

"Horsehair was commonly stirred into the plaster before application for the same general reason, to make it hold better. The idea was to give it resistance to cracking and make it hold together better. Some plasterers used it, and some did not. I expect, like today, there were different qualities of plaster and plasterers. Maybe the horsehair was added to the lower quality, for it needed a little help to hold up and be solid. Or maybe, just like today, there just were differences of opinion among the various craftsmen."

Meg went on up the stairs and commented as we entered the upstairs hallway, "Look, you can see here in these long walls the same pattern of putting a section at an angle for about ten feet in the middle and then returning to the horizontal pattern. You think that was done for better stability of the plaster?"

"Exactly. Look at this bare wall you or your crew just stripped. Look behind the lathe and see the round pieces of plaster?"

"I see them. That must be the part of the plaster that oozed between slats to hold it tightly. That is amazing! I get more and more excited every time we discuss another aspect of my wonderful house. Oh, that reminds me, don't let me forget to show you an unusual pattern in the lathe, not at all like what we see here. It is downstairs near the fireplace. I know it will intrigue you."

"What's the oddity?"

"Well, just that some of the lathe was missing in one spot. But we'll look when we get back down there."

Meg walked down the wide hall while I considered why any house built before wheelchair access requirements would have a six-foot-wide hallway.

"Getting back to our discussion downstairs." Meg's voice brought me back to our conversation. "Here is that upper door to the outside," she said as we reached the opposite end of the hall.

"Wait for a moment on that." I motioned to the right. "You tore out an old bathroom here, correct? See the different floor materials here as opposed to those in the hall?"

"You're suggesting again this is evidence of a different use in former times. You think the maid's stair would have come up here?"

"That's what I think."

"But this seems to be such a wasted space. The stair didn't take up all this room, did it?"

"I doubt it. Remember, there also would have been an upstairs pantry. The maid would have had cupboards upstairs for all the blankets, towels, and bedding, including sheets and pillowcases. Maybe she would store extra mattress ticks here."

"Ticks? The little biting critters? Yuck." Meg shivered just thinking about it.

"No! A tick was the covering of a mattress. It would be the bag part that would then be filled with a variety of materials. They were filled with material as simple as straw or as fancy as goose-down.

Sometimes, as a tick would begin to wear out, another cover would be made and slipped over the old one. So I suggest there might have been some spare ticks here in some upstairs pantry's cupboard."

"That sounds like what we call a linen closet today."

"Exactly, I think a line of cabinets here with blankets and linens would have been the family's linen closets. Realize also this pantry was positioned to be accessible to the maid who did the work, not the family. So it would be by the maid's stair, and on the other side of the hall would be her bedroom."

Meg looked into the small room. She sighed, as if imagining how a person could live in such sparse quarters, take care of all the bedrooms, and go up and down doing the kitchen chores. She finally commented disgustedly, "This is the smallest room up here. That seems obviously prejudiced."

"Definitely, for you see, domestic labor was pretty much the bottom of the labor chain, even if we're not in the South with out-and-out slavery."

"That seems so odd to me. The maids had rather important responsibilities, like cooking, cleaning, and as you now point out up here, making all the beds and such."

"Yes, very true. Like this door here." I moved to open a door that opened out of the maid's room to another room.

"What does that door have to do with the maid?"

"Don't you think it odd that this larger bedroom would have its own door to the maid's room?" I asked Meg.

"I had assumed these two rooms were more like the maid's apartment. But I can tell by your grin and the twinkle in your eye that there is more here than I am seeing."

"I'll bet this larger bedroom was the nursery. Who do you think took care of the children, if there were any?"

I could see wheels turning in Meg's head. That was a quality I admired in her. She was a good thinker.

I continued, "On top of her many other activities, a maid may have been a nanny too."

Meg sighed. “I was thinking it was a graciously large suite-like apartment for the maid. Now I see what you mean by the heavy demands made on these women. Although I admire many of the aspects of living in those years, I am glad I am here in this time, not theirs.”

We both stopped and thought about what Meg had said. I too had probably romanticized those days. As we explored the renovation project together, I think we were appreciating and respecting them more.

“Seldom would the maid have had more than a small room. This house has these three bedrooms upstairs, which are not a lot for a house of this stature. If children were raised here, there were two for children and one for parents. That was one reason why porches were so important, especially in the summer. Therefore, at the back of the house, out this door near the maid’s room, would be a porch.”

“That’s hard for me to imagine now, for this door goes nowhere. It doesn’t even have a stairway down to the backyard.”

“But remember the pattern of the old stair your carpenters found on the back wall? It would have come up here.”

Meg grinned. “I do like the summer porch idea we talked about. I have driven around town like you suggested and have seen several examples of what you describe.”

“But the rear porch still doesn’t solve one basic problem. For a house this large and this fancy, with a maid and all, there still were only three bedrooms up here.”

Meg spoke the very question I, too, had been considering. “Doesn’t that seem a bit odd for a house like this?”

Considering Meg’s last question, I walked again out to the wide hallway. “No third floor,” I sort of mumbled under my breath.

“A third floor?” the sharp-eared Meg asked.

“Yes, don’t you think it is odd about the window? Remember when we were talking about the defining qualities of this old house, we talked of the two leaded-glass windows?”

“Yes, one is here in the front room. I love this room and imagine a bright sitting room with the morning sun beaming in this raised leaded window. I'd have a desk here by this side window. Then I could look out and see the people coming and going outside. Pine Street would have been a fairly main street then. Don't you agree?"

"Oh, yes. But where is the second leaded window?"

Meg looked around somewhat bewildered as I continued. "The window is on the third floor," I said as I pointed to the ceiling.

"But how do we get there?"

"I don't know. You're the carpenter on this house."

"Now you've got me intrigued. Why is there no stairway?" We walked out into the wide hall and stopped. She looked at me suspiciously, and said, "Do you think…?"

"I sure do. This hall was not six feet wide originally. Old houses are famous for narrow doorways and narrow halls."

Questions began to tumble out as Meg cut me off in midthought. "Could there have been a stairway here? Which direction? Would it have come from the rear or from the front? Why is it gone? Why would it be removed? What's up there? How do we get there?"

"Now you've got a mystery, Mrs. Sherlock Holmes. All I know is that there is a leaded-glass window up there and no stairway to get to it."

~

Chapter 8

Year 1891

Spring was indeed a welcome sight for those who had endured the long Michigan winter. The snow piles were melting. Tulips and hyacinths joined the crocuses and daffodils peeping up through the ground, especially along the south edges of house foundations. But for the domestic worker, that meant a heavy workload of spring cleaning. The dust and soot were a constant presence in a city where wood and coal were the heating fuels. Also, most streets were only dirt or gravel paths from which the horses and buggies rolled up constant dust as soon as they dried out from the snow. In the spring it was either muddy and wet or dry and dusty; dirt seemed to get everywhere.

"I have so much to do now that the windows can be opened. I will get Phillip to remove the shutters

from the upper porch so I can air things out. Then I can clean those neglected places where the dust bunnies live." Priscilla smiled at her joke. She did love her work, and the spring freshness inspired her. As she stepped out on that upper summer porch, she was reminded that even with the sun shining and the temperatures of spring rising, Lake Michigan always kept Muskegon cooler than inland cities. She pulled her sweater close around her neck.

Her mind wandered, and she began to smile. *Tomorrow is Sunday,* she thought, and that thought warmed her through.

~

The city was a lumbering town but only for six days a week. The lure of lumber brought a rich variety of people to the area. And along with them, they, of course, brought their ethnic backgrounds, their customs, and obviously, their churches. Churches dotted the area. The earliest Protestant Meeting House was built about 1840, and the Catholics, namely one Father Visosky, came from Grand Rapids and held mass in a home in 1835. The building and establishment of congregations followed quickly, with the Methodist Church dedicated in 1859, a Congregational Church in 1864, and the Unitarian Church in 1865. St. Paul's

Episcopal congregation was established in 1866, although a building was not built until 1875.

On this spring morning, Miss Addy Driscoll was escorted to church with her new friend, Mr. Petronius Frisk, whom everyone called Peter.

"Good morning, Miss Driscoll. Have I met your friend before?" Father Van Grough asked.

"It is good to see you this morning, Father. This is my friend Peter, who is from Chicago and staying in our city for a while."

Addy introduced Peter to a family as they were chatting after services at St. Mary's Catholic Church on Clay and Jefferson. This large church had been started in 1856 by Irish descendents. Other Catholic congregations also reflected their ethnic backgrounds, such as the French at St. Jean, the Baptiste, the Polish at St. Michaels, the Germans at St. Josephs, etc. Peter had been attending with Addy especially since the tensions had risen over the death of her father.

Originally, Addy's father, Terence Driscoll, had worked for one of the mill owners as the chief accountant. He had worked hard at all aspects of the lumber business. His wife's sickness and sudden death twenty years earlier had devastated him. He had used the family money he'd gotten from her death to wisely invest in several successful business ventures. Recently, Addy had sensed tenseness in her father. He never seemed satisfied. His death had been a shocking blow to Addy. There was a shroud of unanswered questions that had troubled Addy greatly. Mr. Frisk had been a good companion during these difficult times.

It was a crisp but sunny spring morning, and everyone was so tired of winter they did not notice the temperature, only the smell of springtime in the air. St. Mary's had started to build a convent and a school north of the church building. The congregation deeply believed in education of the frontier children and looked forward to an operating school soon.

Father Patrick's service was uplifting, and Addy spent much time at the kneeler working through her grief. Peter wanted to reach out, but Victorian customs and his shyness forced him to sit near and only watch her struggle.

As they left the service, Father came over to Addy and took her hand. "How are ya doin', girl?" he asked in his heavy accent. He was a tall man with wavy blond hair and large hands. Her hand felt secure in his as he spoke so tenderly. Their eyes met. Tears were evident in Addy's gaze, but she was composed.

"Oh, thank you, Father, for asking. We are as well as we can be. My father taught me to be strong to survive the harsh realities of this pioneer life. I feel his strength near me daily."

"Yes, I am sure you do, my dear. Your papa was so darn proud of you and commented to me often what a capable woman you'd grown to be."

Addy and Peter thanked Father Van Grough and moved on outside. Then a voice interrupted their quiet reflection.

"Oh, Addy? It is so good to see you." Priscilla was bubbling as she rushed up to her friend. "You look lovely today, and the day is so fresh with spring."

"Dearest Priscilla. How have you been? You've been working far too much, for you have not been around to see me. Shame on you." Addy jested with Priscilla as they fell into a close embrace.

"You know how Mr. Wallace is!" Priscilla explained. "Mrs. Wallace and I have been out regularly to shop, but we've also spent much of our time packing, for we may move."

A quick glance of interested surprise passed between Addy and Peter while Priscilla gushed on.

Peter especially took note of the name Wallace. He thought, *Where did I just see that name? Oh, yes, on those deeds. A very interesting connection indeed.* However, he kept his thoughts to himself.

Priscilla continued, "I had hoped I would run into you on one of our errands. I know you have been consumed working on your own matters with the estate business and all." Priscilla's head dropped, as she was embarrassed to have even obliquely brought up the death of Addy's father. "Oh, I'm sorry," she muttered.

"Oh, Priscilla dear, don't be so glum. Your lovely spirit and smile are just what I needed to remind me of the joys of my life today. I'm with my friends, my church, and this community I love so dearly." Peter looked down and shuffled his feet as the two ladies chatted. "Oh, Mr. Frisk. I am so rude. Priscilla, this is my new friend Peter, Mr. Petronius Frisk. Mr. Frisk is from Chicago and is an insurance investigator for the Chicago Fire Insurance Company."

"Pleased to meet you, sir," Priscilla said and curtseyed politely.

"The pleasure is mine, Miss Priscilla. To meet such a beautiful friend of Addy's is definitely an honor for me."

Priscilla blushed and turned to beckon Alex to join their conversation. As Alex approached, he caught Peter's eye, and a note of recognition passed between them. "This is my dear friend, Alex Hillman. Alex, this is my adopted sister, Miss Addy Driscoll, and her friend Mr. Frisk.

"I am so pleased to meet you, Miss Driscoll." Alex took her hand and bowed respectfully.

"Such a dear gentleman your friend is," Addy whispered and winked at the shy Priscilla, who continued to blush and giggle.

"Mr. Frisk." Alex offered his hand. Peter shook it and smiled.

"Alex and I have met," Peter added. "It is good to see you here, sir. By the way, I got your note last night when I returned to my room. What is this exciting thing you are so pressed to share?"

Alex glanced around uneasily. The two ladies stood there with astonished looks on their faces. "You two know each other?" Addy queried.

"We met at Mrs. Charlton's rooming house," Peter explained, filling in the blank. "Alex works at one of the mills I had dropped in at some days back. He helped me get the lay of the land, you might say. Thank you again, Alex, for your kind assistance and clear directions. Thanks to your help, I've been able to get around quite well."

"Pleasure is mine, Mr. Frisk. I admire the work you do. I too would like to work in Chicago one day and undertake these adventurous investigations like you."

"Oh, hold on now. Most adventures, as you call them, are a lot of tedious walking, asking questions, and paperwork—over and over. More work than adventure most of the time, I'm afraid. But let's not waste these beautiful ladies' time. We will connect tonight. About eight o'clock all right with you?"

Alex nodded in agreement. "I'll meet you out in front of the inn."

"Now, ladies, spring weather or not, we must be going." Peter was gracious and polite as he helped Addy into her carriage.

"Thank you for the well wishes, Priscilla," Addy called back to her friend. "It was also nice to meet you, Alex."

As the carriage moved away, Priscilla turned to Alex. "Aren't you the mysterious one? Having a meeting with some important Chicago investigator, are you? Tell me. Tell me. What are you about?"

"Oh, you are too curious for your own good," Alex chided her. "None of your business. Not yet anyway," he muttered under his breath.

Not to be put off or outdone, she replied, "Everything about you is my business, Mr. Alexander." She coyly cocked her head, and those eyes and that smile melted all his tough resolve and distant musings.

"Come." Taking Priscilla's arm, he invited her to walk with him. "Let's take the long way back to Pine Street. Do you have some time?"

"For you," she said, "I always have time." She said it with enough warmth to heat up the coolest spring breeze coming in off the lake. Even though the spring air was warming, Muskegon Lake gave coolness to the breeze. She pulled her wrap closer and tucked her arm around his elbow as they walked toward downtown.

Alex began to tell her his thoughts. "You know Peter was brought here to investigate the suspicious fire that destroyed the James's mill last month, don't you? Many believe, or at least there are plenty of rumors, that the fire was purposely set to collect the insurance money."

"No!" Priscilla responded dramatically. "Can Mr. Frisk prove that?"

"He is having a lot of difficulty because so many folk are dependent on big-money mill owners like Mr. James or Mr. Smithson. Some men have been hired to follow and discourage Peter. He had a small altercation the other day at the inn, where a man tried to pick a fight, but Mrs. Charlton stepped in and shooed the man out, threatening him with her broom. I watched this happen as I was just returning from work at the mill. The man went outside and was joined by another larger man named Pattone who I have seen around our mill. He is mean and has a bad reputation among the men. I worry that he and his buddy will try to do Peter more harm. But I also know Peter is no stranger to fighting; he can handle himself. He may walk with a bit of a limp and seem to favor one arm, but don't let that fool you. I watched him when that man confronted him. He was stony and steady. When the man reached for a bottle to swing at him, Peter grabbed the man's arm, and the man cringed in pain. No, Peter is a man among men."

"You deeply admire him, don't you?" Priscilla asked.

"Yes. He has been very nice to me. Like today, when he publicly thanked me in front of your influential friend, Miss Driscoll."

"I could see you stand taller as he spoke. I'm also proud of you, Alex. You are very perceptive and take in all the details you see around you. Perhaps you should be a writer and write a history of our area someday."

Alex squeezed her hand as they exchanged smiles. Then he went on with his story. "I noticed something the other day when I met Phillip at Geordie's Livery. Phillip was worried about a problem with Mr. Wallace's buggy. As Geordie was fixing it, he dug out a kind of marl—"

"What is that?" she interrupted.

"It's a kind of slippery clay that you find sometimes along the water's edge. He dug it out of the hub, and I recognized it as being from the swamp hole behind Mr. Wallace's big mill. That is the only place in this area you can find that blue-green type of marl. But the question is, *what was Mr. Wallace doing down in that area?* I think Peter can help sort out some of this mystery. That's why I asked him to meet me this evening."

"Alex, you won't be in danger, will you? If you're concerned with Peter's safety, I don't want to have to worry about your safety."

"No concern, my dear. Now let's not be so serious. It's a beautiful day, in beautiful weather, in our beautiful city, and I'm with a beautiful companion. Now we're off to a beautiful Sunday dinner with the Wallaces."

"Yes! Mr. Wallace said he'd be sure to be home today, so we must all be prompt and on our best behavior."

"I've been concerned and watching him lately as he comes and goes at his mill. He seems to be under a lot of stress. And he seems distracted about something. Do you see the same at home?"

"He has not been around the house very much lately. Seems to come and go at late hours. Phillip was complaining about Mr. Wallace just yesterday. He said Mr. Wallace had called him out at such odd hours lately to get a buggy ready or to put one away."

"I don't mean to sound suspicious, but keep your eyes open."

"Alex?" Priscilla paused as she got serious and thoughtful. "I'm sure it's nothing but... Well, I was upstairs doing my spring cleaning the other day. I was taking some things out to the summer porch and sweeping away the winter's collection of cobwebs. I can't believe how a place can collect so much dirt. It must be the wind blowing through the screens that brings so much dust. I hung the washed mattress ticks up to air and dry, and I believe they were as dirty when they dried as they were when I hung them up."

"Priscilla," Alex interrupted. "You were going to tell me something?"

"Oh, yes. I nearly forgot."

Just then they turned the corner at Clay and Third Street. They were both startled by the sound of a frustrated driver and his team. It was a beautiful team of black horses, not heavy horses, just the kind for a nice carriage. But the driver was yelling and driving them hard. He cracked a whip as he sped down the nearly empty street. Alex looked after the wagon in disgusted interest.

"Why does anyone need to hurt horses that way?" Priscilla spoke with the compassion she always felt for animals. Mr. Wallace had scolded her recently for feeding the dog, Wally, too many scraps out the back door of the kitchen. Her mind wandered at that thought. *Why was Mr. Wallace so sensitive about his dog and so cruel to everyone else?* Alex's voice brought her back to the present.

"That is the same big man I spoke of earlier, Louie Pattone," Alex muttered, also disgusted at the shameful treatment of that beautiful team. "Now, you were telling me something before we were interrupted by the confusion."

"Oh, yes. I was on the summer porch. I didn't want to appear like a snoop, but they were talking so loudly!"

"Who?" queried Alex.

"I looked out into the rear yard when I heard them. I didn't see anybody. I thought the voices might be coming from the stable."

"Who was talking, Priscilla? Get on with your story! You are driving me crazy with anticipation."

"Oh, Alex, you are so impatient." She pouted coyly at him. Then she continued. "I recognized Mr. Wallace's voice and one other man. Mr. Wallace was talking loudly and motioning at the other man with his finger as he insisted on his point. All I could understand was him saying, 'I don't want you coming here to my home again. I'll meet you behind the mill when we're ready.' The other man was a large man dressed as a woodsman, but he was partially hidden behind the tree."

Alex interjected, "That sounds like Pattone's friend. I think his name is Shelvay or Slevey, something like that anyway. When did this happen, Priscilla?"

"It was Thursday, the day before we saw you downtown."

"Yes, and the day before Phillip took the buggy to Geordie's with the marl in the hub." Alex seemed to drift off in thought as their walk neared Pine Street.

"I must meet Peter tonight, I think…" He stopped in midsentence.

Priscilla pinched his arm and said, "Well, go on! You never finish your sentences either. Do you know how much that bothers me?"

"Oh, don't fret Priscilla! We're nearly home, and I'm sure dinner will be wonderful. I must admit, I am always a bit uneasy around Mr. Wallace. He is really my boss too, even though I report to Mr. Smithen, the office manager. I doubt if Mr. Wallace will even recognize that I work in the mill office. But I especially enjoy being with your Mrs. Wallace. She is so dear and kind. You're lucky to have such a considerate boss."

"On some days it's hard to think of her as my boss. We talk and work together often as friends. I enjoy Mrs. Wallace's insights and her caring attitude toward others. She is so thoughtful, not rough or loud like Mr. Wallace."

"We're almost back to the house," Alex shared as he patted Priscilla's hand. "Let's enjoy the rest of today. We'll try to not let all these other concerns get in the way."

Priscilla agreed, but Alex gave away his feelings as he drifted back into his thoughts: "*...the buggy, the marl, the rough team driver, and the investigator. Could Priscilla's Mr. Wallace be involved in this mess? And how?*" His thoughts raced.

Phillip had tethered the horse and carriage at the front of the house. But Phillip was nowhere in sight; Alex was thinking of asking him more questions about the buggy and Mr. Wallace's unusual outing the past Thursday night.

"Hello, Alex." The dear, sweet voice interrupted his musings. "I hope you are hungry," Mrs. Wallace declared as she opened the door and invited the young couple into her home.

~

Chapter 9

Year 2000

"There is no access to the third floor, but the builder I hired did put a ladder up to the outer window one day not too long ago. He was able to move the sash and climb in for a closer look."

"I know, I know, and he found the gold hidden there? Or did he find a skeleton or something really spooky?"

"A treasure? I wish. I'm not that lucky. But we did find something in the basement you'd be interested to see. You'll remember this house was generally clean when I bought it."

"I know that very well. Remember? I was the contractor who was hired by your real estate friend to change the locks and clean it out. And you're correct, there was very little or nothing left in here. There were just a few old boxes, and I remember some old shelves in the dining room used to display the previous owner's artwork. Remember her paintings on the walls?"

"Oh, yes, the flowers and vines. Interesting but gaudy. Not sure I'd call it art."

"I remember some wood and a couple old bed frames in a corner of the basement. How could I have missed something? There was so little there in the first place. So, what mystery did you uncover?"

"Come downstairs. I have it in the kitchen."

We descended the stairs, again marveling at the gorgeous oak woodwork. As we passed through the living room with the beautiful mantel piece, we both paused.

Meg said, "Don't get sidetracked here, but remind me, I do have a question to ask you about this area."

"Great, I love a good puzzle. So where is your basement treasure?"

"Here. I set it in this makeshift cabinet that I put in the kitchen just to store tools." She carefully opened the upper cupboard door, knowing the cabinet was not fastened to the wall. She explained that she had tipped it over the day before and spilled her drywall tools all over the floor. She wasn't worried about the tools, she explained, "But I was concerned not to break this."

She handed me a lantern. It was a kerosene type, but the globe had been cracked. It was plenty rusty, as you'd expect a lantern left in an old basement to be.

"We didn't find it right away," she explained. "My workers found it only after they opened a piece of floor on the first floor. It was sort of hidden under the floorboards. Jim was so excited that he ran clear upstairs where I was working to show it to me. We'd all joked as we removed plaster and began rehabbing that we hoped we'd find a hidden treasure behind some secret wall. No gold, unfortunately, only this rusty lantern."

"It was always the same with me. My goal was always to find a Wells Fargo box full of Morgan silver dollars from the Carson City Mint," I shared. "So it was with my crew; they were always out to find a treasure. But yours is a treasure. Did you find any names or dates on it?" I inquired as I turned it upside down myself to investigate.

“No apparent marks, but I intended to do some gentle steel wool work on it when I get a chance.” Meg watched carefully as I examined the lantern closely in the light.

“I was expecting this to be a general-purpose farm lantern or maybe a railroad lantern. Railroad lantern glass was usually red or green and used by the brakemen or the caboose operator for obvious signals of stop or go. But this one is different.”

“Oh! How is that?” Meg asked.

“This one has this shield or deflector piece. It wasn’t used for general lighting. For that kind of use, you’d want the light spread in all directions, to light the whole yard or a whole room. No, this one was hung somewhere like on a door, or on a wall, or maybe on the back of a wagon.”

“I sort of see what you mean. It’s made so the light only shines in one direction. But I don’t understand why.”

I thought for a moment and then responded.

“Today, for example, we might have a porch light at the side of the door. It only shines out and is shielded on the back so as to not overheat the wood siding.”

"OK, I get that, but what did you mean about using it on a wagon?"

"I may have misled you with the term wagon, for I was actually thinking more of a covered buggy or a carriage. A lantern might be hung on the back, like the taillight you and I have on our cars and vehicles now."

"I must say, your family background with horses and all helps for me get an understanding, not just about the structure of my old house but of how the people lived in it as well. That clears up a lot."

I stammered and stuttered a bit. I thanked her for her graciousness and assured her I was not expert, but I sure did enjoy speculating about the past. I went on.

"I don't know how they kept these old houses or barns from burning down while using lanterns like these. It seems it would have been incredibly easy to tip or kick it over. Then it would be poof, and the entire building would go up in flame.

"Oh yes, like Mrs. O'Leary's cow that started the Great Chicago Fire in 1871?"

I smiled and did not say anything, but Meg caught the gleam in my eye.

"What? You have another theory about the Chicago fire? You don't like the O'Leary Barn Theory?"

I just smiled, recalling a conversation I'd had recently with a friend. We had talked about this very subject but with the added suggestion that fires were often started to collect insurance. I'd told him about the Muskegon Sawdust Fire of 1891. He had commented on how the Muskegon Sawmills had boomed because they supplied the lumber for the rebuilding of Chicago.

"Wouldn't it be interesting if there was a connection?" I asked with a smile and a raised eyebrow.

"I think you just love to build on old conspiracy theory stories and turn them into mysteries." Meg smiled and laughed, chiding me a little bit.

"Who knows? I might have to have my friend write a book sometime about the Muskegon Chicago Connection of the 1800s. Much is agreed on and is recorded history, but the rest—"

Meg interrupted and finished my sentence with, "The rest is your overactive imagination. You think too much. Speaking of dates, look at this. We uncovered it when we cleared the plaster out of this closet."

Meg and I moved over to the wall, which was actually between the kitchen and the dining room. "Look at this heat vent," Meg offered, pointing to the metal flue in the exposed wall.

"Well, that's certainly not an original in this house."

Meg nodded in agreement. "But I wonder if it wasn't the first attempt to get central heat into the house. Here this is what I wanted you to see." She pointed down to the manufacture's plate on the side of the register boot. The label read:

Sterling Metal Fabricating

Manufactured: 1898

Chicago, Ill.

"That's a fascinating date."

"How so?"

“It indicates this heating system was put in around the turn of the century. That fits because of the date of the fire.”

“You’ve spoken of that fire before.”

“Yes, I am referring to what has been named the Pine Street Fire. It occurred in 1891. The fire started near downtown and went south down Pine Street. The wind changed, and it burned back north on Pine Street to burn out in Muskegon Lake. It did that in one short day. The Chicago fire we just spoke of took three days to do its damage.”

I could see Meg getting very thoughtful. Then she asked, “So how old is this house?”

“I am quite sure the original house would have burned that day in May of 1891. Back then, homes owned by richer persons may have been insured, so they might have been rebuilt more quickly and often on the same spot. So it fits that this house may have been rebuilt around 1900 or just before.”

“Do you think that explains its quality and style?” Meg asked.

“It may explain the quality and being able to be rebuilt but especially would explain the installation of central heat at such an early date. People with money were able to rebuild. And like people today, they often wanted to show off by installing the latest convenience. Central heating would represent a big improvement. When they rebuilt after the devastating fire, they could incorporate this new invention, central heat, not just rebuild what an older home, say built in the 1860s, might have had.

"Also consider the effort of men working in frontier areas to overbuild their houses to convince their reluctant wives and families to move to the edge of civilization and leave their comfortable big-town homes, say in Chicago. I heard one story about a man who discovered the silver in Virginia City, Nevada. It was so remote and desolate, he had a twenty-five-room mansion built and had a mirror gilded with diamond dust to lure his wife there away from of San Francisco. That is sure going to extremes in spending money."

"Really not all that different than from today, I'm afraid," Meg added with a sigh. "Be assured there will be no diamond dust mirrors here."

Chapter 10

Year 1891

That evening, Alex was sitting on the bench out in front of Charlton's Inn. Since it was Sunday, the lumber workers were enjoying their only day off. The bar area inside the inn was crowded, and voices were loud. An occasional argument even drew a punch or two, but it was generally pretty still, with the regulars coming and going. Three old-timers sat at the bench on the other side of the front door, slouched down, telling stories and spitting tobacco into the street.

There was not much carriage traffic today. The inn was near the mills. During the week, a steady number of supply wagons with their teams and workmen moved past. Today was quiet, traffic wise.

Peter startled Alex as he approached. "Mr. Alex, I hope you haven't been waiting long. I'm sure you enjoyed today's dinner with the pretty Miss Priscilla. Yes?"

Alex jumped up to see Mr. Frisk's broad smile. He felt a bit nervous but honored just to talk to him.

"It's a nice evening," Peter observed, looking toward the reddening horizon. "Mind if we walk a bit? My leg stiffens up when I sit a spell, and I've spent most of the day sitting."

They walked from the inn to the corner of Pine and Clay and then turned north toward the mill area. They did not talk at first. Being shy, Alex was hesitant to start the conversation. There was so much he wanted to tell Peter and so much he wanted to learn from him. He was relieved when Peter spoke.

"So, Alex, where is this marl pit you told me about?"

Alex's head snapped toward Peter. "How did you know about the marl connection?"

Peter laughed, especially amused that he had surprised his new young friend. "Asking questions and talking to folks is my business. Remember?"

"What about the marl?" Alex stammered.

"You made an excellent observation as a young investigator. You get the credit. I confess I talked to Geordie at the livery just after you and Phillip were there the other day. Geordie is pretty sharp also. Don't let that Scottish brogue or ever-present stump of cigar fool you. He is a keen observer of people and notices many things. I'm pleased he's had some trust in me and has talked openly; many in the town have not. Tell me, Alex, about the marl."

"It started with Phillip's concern about his boss, Mr. Wallace's, odd comings and goings. On Thursday last, Phillip became concerned about the condition of the buggy when he noticed the wobbly wheel as he harnessed up the rig to take Mrs. Wallace shopping for the day. After dropping the ladies downtown, he wisely went directly to Geordie's to have it checked. Geordie accused young Phillip of speeding on the rough corduroy. Of course, Phillip insisted his innocence. Then Geordie dug the marl out of the hub. I know of only one source for that blue-green clay, and that is down behind the Wallace/Smithson Mill, where the sluice pond was originally fed from the Muskegon River."

"Hold on a minute. You are ahead of me. Just so I'm sure, clarify what a sluice pond is," Peter interrupted.

"Some folk call it a soak hole. Regardless, most mills bring their logs into a pondlike area where the logs can be more easily positioned to catch the cogs of the elevator belt that pulls them up to the saws. Men can maneuver them with their pike poles, and some like to walk the logs just like the river loggers do. Often this is a yucky mess of a pond, and the workers will challenge one another to a log-rolling contest. The incentive to stay on the log is high because of that murky, mucky water.

"Anyway," Alex continued, "marl is not a common soil, and it is not found just anywhere. Oh, yes, and most marl is gray, but this one is distinctively blue. My question was: Why was Mr. Wallace down in that area at all? The mill road is not a carriage-type road, for it is very rough and usually only used by big teams dragging logs about."

Peter stopped walking. "Alex, exactly where can this marl be found?" They had stopped near the mill area as they neared the lake.

They were on a slight rise, so they could overlook the mill area. Alex pointed to the right, where the yard was piled high with cut lumber. Large piles of slab cuttings were obvious all along the edge of the mill property. Slab wood was the first cut made on the log to remove the rounded bark and begin to cut the dimensional boards.

"The marl is just beyond the slab piles along a swampy area that leads back toward the lake," Alex said, pointing it out to Peter.

"Hmmm." Peter scratched his head. "Tell me more about your concerns about your boss's activities."

"Well," Alex continued, "Priscilla was telling me—"

Peter interrupted, "By the way I could tell when we were introduced this morning at St. Mary's, she's real sweet on you."

Alex smiled knowingly but returned quickly to the seriousness of his report to Peter. "Anyway, she shared with me information about a visitor who came late Thursday night to Mr. Wallace's private office. Most recently she heard that same man's voice again. She told me she was cleaning the upstairs summer porch and heard Mr. Wallace speaking harshly to a man in the rear yard. She recalled the voice. It was a harsh, mean voice, and I think you know who owns it."

"I know him?" Peter replied with a perplexed look on his face.

"Yes. I watched your confrontation with some man picking a fight with you at the inn some weeks back."

"Was that the man?"

"No. But when that fellow left the inn, I was standing outside on the porch. He was joined by a large man who also was watching you. The big man waiting there was angry with the fellow you fought. He pushed him around some. They walked off together arguing."

"The man watching us, was he tall and broad and wearing a printed sash for a belt?"

"Why, yes. That describes him."

Peter went on to elaborate. "Yes, he's been following me around town. He followed me the other day when I walked to the baseball field across the flats to see a game. I don't fear him, but I'd like to know who he's working for."

Alex replied, "He works as a log puller at Wallace and Smithson's mill."

“Oh, he does, does he?” Peter mused, rubbing his chin in contemplation.

“That’s the mill right there” Alex continued. “His name is Pattone, and I think his first name is Jake or Jack.”

Peter pulled a piece of paper from his pocket and began to write a note. “Do you spell that name p-a-t-t-o-n-e?”

“Yes, that’s correct,” Alex said.

“Was there another incident today? You seemed upset at dinner today.”

“Yes. Another thing happened today as Priscilla and I were walking back to the Pine Street House after church. We were startled by a racing, puffing team. We had just turned the corner at Third Street when this angry driver, yelling at a beautiful team of black carriage horses, came around the corner with a mill wagon. I recognized it, for it had the mill’s brand and symbol on the front corner. He is such a mean driver.”

“I think he’s mean to everyone and everything,” Peter added.

"There was another thing about the buggy. When the ladies pulled away after their shopping the other day, I noticed a lantern mark on the rear of the buggy."

"What is a lantern mark?" Peter asked.

"Well, when a lantern is hung on the rear at night so as to be seen by other traffic, it swings to and fro to the motion of the buggy. As it swings, it makes a mark, sort of an arch-shaped wear in the wood."

"So?"

"I guess it is just a coincidence," Alex muttered, doubting Peter was very interested.

"Remember, Alex, when you are investigating something, nothing is coincidence. You are great at taking in details. Maybe they are random pieces right now, but eventually they may fit in and help us complete this puzzle."

Alex smiled and enjoyed Peter's encouragement, so he went on. "Well, it's about the lantern. Phillip… you remember he tends the Wallace's' stable? Well, Phillip was mentioning about the lantern. Mr. Wallace demands his lanterns be kept polished. But the rear lantern was so dirty, even mud spattered when Mr. Wallace came back late Thursday evening. Phillip was grumbling at the difficulty he had in cleaning it. I recall it was a directional lantern. I mean it had a shield on one side so it could hang against the wood of the rear seat and not burn it. That was the lantern Phillip would light to guide people into the buggy even when there were sidelights, like on Mr. Wallace's fancy four-seater buggy. The lantern then would be hung on the rear of the buggy as it pulled away. The process would be reversed when they returned. The servant or helper would first grab the rear lantern, then open the door of the buggy and help the guests down, lighting a path for them."

Alex continued to educate the interested and attentive Peter. "Mr. Wallace's lantern is unique. A couple of nights ago, I was out in front of the inn talking to Homer Elkins, a coworker at the mill. There was just the normal traffic of people and rigs. As we talked, a buggy went hurrying by. What I remembered was this special shiny brass lantern swaying on the rear."

"Are you suggesting you recognized the buggy?"

"I think so. And now I remember it was going down toward the mill. Then, the next day at Geordie's, and the marl in the hub, and—"

"Hold on. Hold on. Don't get ahead of yourself. Just help me put the pieces together like an investigator."

"Do you think it is all connected?"

"I'm not sure yet, my young friend. But you've been a big help. You and Priscilla keep your eyes open and let me know if you discover anything else. I have some paperwork to get in the mail to my boss in Chicago. He believes there's more going on here than just accidental fires."

"Peter, I thank you for your patience. I'll surely see you in the next few days."

As the two men were shaking hands and saying their good-byes, two large wagons rumbled by them. Both wagons were labeled with the same Wallace-Smithson Mill brand name. Curiously, the wagons were piled high with furniture and loaded down with belongings. The drivers kept the teams going unusually slowly over the rutty cords. Both Peter and Alex looked at each other with the same questioning glance—*why were those wagons so loaded with household goods, and where were they going?*

Alex stared as he recognized the cherrywood china hutch tied to the rear of the first wagon. He gestured to Peter to indicate he recognized the furniture as the Wallace's. He also recalled Priscilla lamenting about the work she and Mrs. Wallace had been doing as they carefully packed all their precious dishes. She and Alex had wondered at the time why the dishes were being packed. Were the Wallaces planning to move soon? Rumors had been heard around the mill daily, but the superintendent vehemently denied any possibility of closing.

As Alex tapped Peter on the arm, he saw Peter's expression turn to a steely cold glare. Alex followed the stare to the second wagon. Peter and the burly driver momentarily locked eyes. Even in the evening darkness, Peter recognized him as his nemesis, Pattone. The wagons turned left, away from the mill. Where were they going?

Peter quickly excused himself and departed. "I think I understand now," he muttered to himself as he hurried to send an urgent wire for his Chicago boss to receive first thing Monday morning.

Chapter 11

Year 2000

As we retraced our steps and came through the kitchen area, Meg spoke up. "Hey, time for a break. Can I interest you in a cup of coffee? I always bring a thermos when I come here to work."

"Yes, I'd love that. Coffee is like the oil that runs my engine. I think I inherited that from my Robotham family. My father carried a coffee maker and Hills Brothers coffee in the trunk of his car like emergency supplies."

Meg found a couple of mugs and poured the coffee. I pulled up a couple of paint-stained old chairs and wiped the seats off with a rag. She brought over the coffee cups and sat them on an upside-down bucket. It was not a very fancy setting but totally functional. As I sat blowing on the hot coffee in my mug, I said to Meg, “Let your imagination wander a bit with me.”

“Oh, yes, like that’s new. You have already stretched my imagination in every way possible already, especially about what life was like in my house.” Meg laughed sarcastically.

I smiled and sipped, knowing she was correct. “Stick with me, please, and try it again. Here we are in this kitchen. The two of us are just taking a break from work. One of us is a member of the family and the other a friend. The woodstove would be over there with a fire burning; it is midday, so the fire was banked, but we would certainly feel the heat. Now maybe there would be a small table over here, or maybe not so small depending on the family size and preference for eating.” I motioned to different spots as I talked, imagining the room a century earlier. “Would it be any different if, say, one of the original family members invited a friend in for coffee back in 1891?”

Meg did not ponder for a second but spoke up. “Well, for starters, I wouldn’t be pouring the coffee from a thermos. And these cookies would not come from a package I bought last night at the store.”

“All that you said would surely be true. What do we know about coffee in 1891? Would it be different?

Stronger? Maybe we would have a small grinder and grind whatever we need? You would pick up the coffee pot off the stove where it may have brewed for hours. Yes, I think stronger. Do you think the people would dunk their cookies?"

Meg opened the cookies, took out several, and handed me the bag. She tried to bite one cookie and then laughed. "Yep, I do think they would dunk these cookies, and so will I."

"My mind wanders to think of it. Would I be dunking peanut butter cookies in 1891? Or maybe we would be at the big Occidental Hotel downtown. I might have to smoke a cigar in those years. Did you know they had a special smoke shop in their hotel? A friend told me once they had a special electric cigar lighter in the outside wall of that shop. You would step up, place the tip of the cigar in this hole, push the button, and it would light." He looked at Meg and laughed. "Well, maybe you wouldn't have lit your cigar there."

She rolled her eyes at my wild idea. "I like the idea of coffee at the hotel. What would we eat there? Not a cookie, but maybe a scone or...I guess I don't know what they served." Meg went on. "By the way, changing the subject slightly, I've been doing some reading in those books you gave me on Muskegon history. They were interesting and taught me a bunch. Every time I would read, I would find myself daydreaming about what it must have been like. The thinking we were just sharing here in this kitchen is exactly what my mind has been doing as I read. I bet the cookies would certainly have been homemade. I own an antique piece of furniture called a pie safe. I bet one of those would have sat on the back porch to cool and protect the pies. I don't know how to even bake a pie. I would have to learn a lot real fast to be able to have survived in 1891."

"A while back, when we talked about the cistern, we spoke of fruit. In one of those books it spoke of Mr. Peck and Mr. Sanford raising apples and grapes in the area close to downtown. The streets Catawba, Delaware, Hartford, and Iona are all named for varieties of grapes."

"That is exciting, for the corner of Hartford and Delaware is almost exactly where my house first sat. I think that makes a great connection linking my house today with the history of the area."

"I did some Internet exploring. Muskegon County was not listed as a major producer of grapes in those days. So these street names are more a product of Mr. Peck's and Mr. Sanford's political input than their huge vineyard."

"I am impressed that you have done so much learning. However, are you sure your great knowledge of grapes and wine may indicate some problem?"

Meg threw me a dark look. I was fearful she might throw something more harmful, so I quickly put up my hands to shield my face. I pled for mercy, and we both laughed. We shared how exciting it was that history lived on. In this case, a vineyard became street names we saw every day as we drove through our neighborhoods.

I said, "The lumber industry is credited with a lot, mostly because of the personal benevolence of Charles Hackley. Remember, most of our, quote, lumber barons, took their money and left. But there were many other names of that time. We spoke of Hackley, Peck, and Sanford, but we should add Moon, McLaughlin, Lyman, and Taylor, along with many others. Later industries, also connected to our lumber heritage, came and shaped our area. One was Brunswick, who used the hardwoods to make bowling lanes. Another was Walker, who made beautiful oak office furniture. You may remember the name Hartshorne. They made the wooden roller insides of window shades."

Meg spoke up, adding, "Yes, I remember reading of some of those people in the book. I also see evidence around town for most of those names. There was one other I'd never heard of, and neither do I see the name anywhere. That name was Goodrich. How do they fit in?"

"They were big in the shipping business. They operated out of Chicago and ran regular steamship routes on the Great Lakes. Remember, this was before there were lots of roads, even before many railroads, so steamer travel was a very popular mode of transportation for many. There schedule was extensive. I have a copy of a picture showing their ship, the Alabama, in dock at their Third Street Dock in Chicago. The schedule on the sign says: *Daily Arrivals—Alabama to Grand Haven/Muskegon at 10:00 a.m.* Because of all the mills around Muskegon Lake, Goodrich had their first docks on Lake Michigan our near the channel from Mona Lake, which was called Black Lake at that time."

She replied, "I also read about the resort hotels built out in that area. That would make sense to have the Goodrich docks there bringing vacationers from Chicago to those hotels. They would have access to the small steamer on Mona, I mean Black Lake, getting folk back to the city. I read that one of the hotels was the Antisdale Hotel. I had a friend that lived on that street off Lake Harbor Road. It is starting to take on new meaning combining today with the history background. I had a question for you that I wondered about: Why steam ships?"

I poured the last of the coffee into our cups and sat back. "Ships have always been the key to growth around the Great Lakes. Simply put, transportation to move any products, in our case mostly lumber, was the key to growth. There was no I-96 through Grand Rapids or any US-31 from Chicago; all we had was the water. There weren't railroads yet, not at least until after the 1891 fire we've been speaking of. Another factor was the fuel. These steamers were powered with wood, making added demand for wood but not milled wood. Many people were employed cutting what was called cord wood and selling it to the steamers that dropped by to fill up just like they would at a gas station today. Oh, speaking of that, I wonder..."

Meg sighed deeply. "Speaking of what, exactly? We've spoken of lots of things."

"What I was thinking of was our tendency to kind of romanticize those years in the previous century. I, for example, love to think of the horses, the teams, and the buggies. I could get off on that. How about you?"

"I don't know if it's romance or not. It might be because I am a woman, but my favorite part of that era is women's dress, especially the hats and the parasols. I don't know what it's about fancy umbrellas, but I love them in the old pictures and movies."

Both of us got quiet and reflective and sipped our coffee. Meg offered me another peanut-butter cookie. I broke it and dunked it, thinking of how this reminded me of my own family.

Meg spoke, "You seemed to have more you wanted to say about the Goodrich ships and the hotels. What was on your mind?"

"You bring up the Goodrich ships, the Lake Harbor Hotel, and that is about all we ever hear about what was going on in that area. However, there was a lot of other activity, and I haven't been able to find any written documentation of that activity."

"You make it sound so sinister or secretive. You have obviously done some research. What do you think?"

"I am sure there was some serious activity there. Some may have been innocent enough. They built the Float Bridge to help the traffic to and from the area, but what kind of activity? Was it just shipping fruit? Hackley's summer cottage and farm was there, and it had a huge boat/storage barn at the lake side. What was he shipping out of there? For another case, have you ever heard of Jonathan Walker, the famous abolitionist? His farm was just west of Hackley's.

"Wasn't he the Man with the Branded Hand?"

"Yes, he's buried right here in Evergreen Cemetery. I do not believe for a minute he stopped his work on the Underground Railroad just because he moved to beautiful Mona Lake. However, I have found no specific records. Mr. Walker moved here from Wisconsin and had done business in Chicago area for the decade before that. There have been plenty of conspiracy theories about Chicago's involvement in Muskegon. Some go way back to the Chicago fire."

"I remember you hinting about that before."

"Again there are no sources to prove that, but there were some forty mills in the area, each with thousands of board feet of lumber stacked on their property. It was not worth a penny, unless there was a demand for it. Guess what? An accidental fire in a town made of wood. I would love to write about this, but in the meantime, I just love a conspiracy."

"You mean there's more to the story? It'll have to wait, for I have other work to do."

Chapter 12

Year 1891

Alex waited anxiously for Peter to arrive. He was not used to setting up meetings at the Occidental Hotel. He looked around and admired the fancy décor. He looked around and did not see him seated anywhere, so he decided to take a seat in the lobby. It was lined with high-backed, soft chairs, with the check-in desk straight ahead from the entrance door. The lounge stretched to his right, with some decorated couches, more chairs, and some big pictures on the walls. As he waited, numerous business owners came and went. Some of those people lived at the hotel, and he wondered how they could afford what appeared to him to be such luxury.

As he sat and watched, three men came in from a large carriage that had delivered them to the door. They were met by Priscilla's boss, Mr. Wallace, who quickly ushered them to a private room off the dining area. Mr. Wallace looked around anxiously as they closed the door. Was he concerned about who might see him? Mr. Wallace had always struck Alex as being nervous and stressed. The man was short and a bit round and had thinning hair, which he nervously passed his hand through often.

About the same time, Marvin Gates, a friend of Alex's, came into the lobby. Seeing Alex, he came over and greeted his friend. Marvin was taller than Alex. He was lanky, and his long black hair indicated his Native American roots. They both looked ill at ease in this place. Alex motioned, and they both sat in the comfortable chairs.

"What are you doing here?" They both seemed to ask the question at the same time and then laughed. Alex spoke first.

"I saw you were driving that big rig that just delivered the three gentlemen."

Marvin seemed to squirm in his chair and looked around with concern. "Where did they go when they came in?"

Alex described how they had been greeted by Mr. Wallace and ushered quickly into the room to the left off the dining area. "You seem to be a bit nervous. What are you concerned about?"

Marvin explained that he had been assigned by Geordie to take the first-class carriage and go to the Goodrich Docks out at Lake Harbor to pick up some passengers. When he arrived at the docks, he waited for the boat to tie up. Soon a man hurried to him, inquiring if he was from Muskegon looking to deliver some businessmen to the Occidental Hotel. The man, who must have been a steward from the Goodrich line, rushed away. He quickly returned with the three gentlemen.

He explained, "After I got them seated in the carriage and closed the door, I asked the steward about their luggage. He looked at me strangely and said there was none. I found that very curious. Then, when I got here to the hotel, one of the men instructed me to stay close, for they were planning to catch the three o'clock boat."

"The three o'clock boat goes to Chicago," Alex added knowingly, for one of the mill owners had had him book passage before.

Marvin relaxed in his chair. "Yes, they are not planning to be here very long. They must be on very important business."

Alex nodded agreement and thought maybe this was another concern Peter might want to know about.

"What are you doing waiting here?" Marvin thought it was just as curious to see Alex, the mill's office manager, sitting in the hotel lobby.

Alex searched for words, not sure what to tell his friend. "I am waiting for a new friend named Peter. We met at the rooming house where I stay. He, too, is from Chicago. He may be interested in knowing about your passengers."

"I am just as curious and afraid I won't be much help, for I don't know—"

Alex interrupted Marvin's comments by placing his hand on his arm and rising. He said, "Hello, Peter. I'm glad you could get here so promptly."

Marvin rose as Peter offered his hand. "Petronius Frisk is my name, young sir."

Marvin shook Peter's hand and nodded, continuing to be a bit confused.

Alex explained, "Marvin works for Geordie and delivered three gentlemen from Chicago here to the hotel. They just arrived by steamer this morning."

Peter looked around the lobby. Alex spoke up. "They went into the small room there"—motioning to his left—"with Mr. Wallace."

"Very interesting," Peter mumbled as he stroked his chin, in a sort of thoughtful mood.

Marvin spoke. "I will leave you two alone. I have to tend to my team anyway; I don't know how long I'll have to wait, but I'll wait with the carriage. It was nice meeting you, Mr. Frisk, and good to see you again Alex." He donned his cap and went out the door.

"Nice chap," Peter commented, and he ushered Alex over to a small table in the café area at the opposite side of the lobby from the dining room. "Let's sit here for a while. Do you want a cup of coffee?"

Alex declined and suggested tea. With Peter's agreement, Alex went to the counter and ordered their tea. He returned to the table with his mind racing, full of questions for Peter.

Peter could see his young friend was anxious to talk but held up his hand to slow his excitement. "Did you get that information I asked you for?" he asked.

Before Alex could answer, the tea was delivered. Peter quickly retrieved a coin from his pocket and paid the waiter.

"I was going to pay for the tea, Peter, but thank you anyway."

Peter nodded, acknowledging his offer with his charming smile, and went back to his question. "Alex, did you make a list for me?"

Alex retrieved a paper from his pocket and handed it to Peter.

Peter opened it and read down the page. "This is very interesting. You are sure one of your bosses went on a trip, most surely to Chicago, on all these dates."

Alex explained that he was usually the one asked to make the travel plans, so his records were surely quite accurate. "What do you want that list for?" Alex inquired.

Peter did not answer quickly and seemed to be turning ideas around in his mind. He then produced another sheet from his own pocket and held them side by side.

"You see, Alex, my list shows a number of times someone from Muskegon came to Chicago over the last year and visited a certain investor my insurance company has had under surveillance."

Alex listened closely and seemed to lean closer to Peter. Alex was very excited to be entering into a real investigation.

Alex was near bursting when he said to Peter. "Peter, these three gentlemen who Marvin just delivered, could they be the Chicago people you might be looking for? If they are, maybe we should call the sheriff or something."

"Whoa, my anxious friend, don't move so fast. Let us enjoy our tea and think this through." With that, they chatted about the possible connections Peter's company had already been investigating that included several other suspicious fires in Saginaw and Holland, as well as in northern Wisconsin. In the town of Peshtigo, on the same day as the Chicago fire, twelve hundred people were killed, five times the number killed in the Chicago disaster. What was most valuable to Peter was to be able to connect certain people in Chicago with certain operations in Muskegon.

As they were chatting, they noticed Geordie's big carriage pull up under the entrance cover at the hotel's front door. Marvin noticed them sitting at the front window of the café area and waved. As they watched, three well-dressed businessmen came out of the hotel and stood for a moment at the carriage talking to another man Peter did not know.

Pointing to the men, Alex told Peter, "Those are the three gentlemen we told you about earlier. The fourth gentleman is Priscilla's boss, Mr. Wallace. I believe he is the silent partner in the Wallace and Smithson Mill where I work." They watched as the men exchanged handshakes and boarded the carriage.

Peter's expression hardened as he looked over the men. Alex noticed Peter getting tense, and he twisted his napkin nervously. Then Alex spoke.

"Do you know any of those men, Peter?"

Peter continued to watch as the carriage pulled away. "The man with the taller hat is a lawyer in a large firm in Chicago. I have suspected that his firm was tangled up in this mess somehow for a long time. I think his name is Hart and his partner's is Johansson, if my memory serves me right."

Peter sat back, and sipped his tea while looking over the two lists. He did not say anything further, and the tension was driving Alex nearly mad.

"Alex, do you know anyone out near the Goodrich docks who we might chat with who would know about the traffic, especially people traffic, who have come and gone regularly?"

As they were speaking, Sam Washoo, Miss Driscoll's Native American friend, came walking past the hotel. Alex jumped up, saying, "I've got an idea." He ran out the front door and hailed the gentleman. As they chatted, Peter came out and joined them. After appropriate introductions, they all smiled and shook hands in agreement.

"That will be excellent, Mr. Washoo. Thank you for offering to introduce me to your niece's husband. What was his name again?"

Alex clarified, "His name is Jacob Randall, and he is the bridge master. He will know everybody who comes and goes in the area. He has lived here for some years, and I believe he even helped build the float bridge. Is that right, Mr. Sam? Oh, is it OK to call you that, sir?"

Mr. Sam Washoo was very well liked in Muskegon. He was a dear friend of Ms. Driscoll's and did odd jobs for her and for her father before he died. "Yes, young man, I answer to both names. Back to the float bridge. Mr. Randall came here alone, I never heard from where. He was hired to choose and survey the area for a bridge. He was befriended by my brother, Black Bow Togobe, who runs a small store out along the south side of Black Lake. That how he met my niece, Ma-wish-in-ga. She is a sister to Black Bow's wife. He will surely help you."

Peter was pleased. "We'll meet you at the livery tomorrow morning at seven. It is about three or four miles out to the bridge area; we should be there in plenty of time to talk and yet return before dark. Mr. Washoo, thank you for riding with me and introducing me to Mr. Randall." Turning to Alex, he said, "I'm sorry you cannot come with us, but I know you need to be back at work tomorrow at the mill."

The next day was very fruitful for Peter. He spent the morning at the bridge, where Jacob explained the operation of the unique structure. Peter watched with amazement as the steamer, *Florence*, approached, blowing her whistle. Jacob jumped to his work: dropping the traffic gates, pulling the pin that allowed the middle floating section of the bridge to move. The water current opened a thirty-foot section, allowing for the steamer to pass through. It was such a quick and fluid operation; Peter quickly grew to respect the wonderful skill of this man everyone seemed to call, with great respect, *The Bridge Master*.

The day seemed quieter after the *Florence* went through, so Jacob and Peter sat and talked some. Jacob had a coffee pot on his small stove in the control shack. The warmth of the spring sun encouraged them to sit outside. The traffic was light, but Peter's questions were many. Jacob explained his story from the beginning.

"I was hired initially to survey the area and recommend where to locate the bridge. I was to clear the area, hire some local crew men, and move on to Manistee for another project. I was captured by the beauty of the area and began to settle. The company then offered me the job of building and overseeing the bridge, and here I am still here." Jacob smiled with a warm grin that made Peter comfortable, and he continued his interview.

Peter, in turn, shared his newly discovered interest in the area. He thanked Jacob for his patient sharing. Peter was the opposite of Jacob. Jacob had lived in the area near twenty years now, so he had lots to learn.

Jacob explained how the orchards and farms had been very productive south of the lake. Production had been excellent, aided by the pleasant shoreline weather, and the fruit seemed to thrive and grow. The growth and popularity of the ships coming and going on the big lake gave the farmers ready access to transport their products to Chicago markets. Everyone gained, and everyone seemed to be happy. Then Jacob grew silent, and it seemed a gloomy cloud drifted over them and their talk.

Peter was sensitive and quickly picked up on his new friend's mood. He asked Jacob a probing question. "What concerns do you have with what you have seen? I will guess far more than fruit has passed your way. Am I getting close to your concerns?"

Jacob continued to look out at the float bridge and relit his pipe. He returned a wave to one of the drivers who crossed with his loaded wagon, heading into town. He exhaled a generous puff of smoke and spoke.

"It is just talk mostly. I try to stay out of the fray, but I listen a lot. For example, there are two major points to the right over there out of sight from the bridge. Lots of goods and people seem to come and go around there. Some of the traffic is late at night. Now what is more suspicious than that kind of activity? We know that many rich Chicago folk love to come here for vacations. The growing hotels out at the big lake encourage that. However, there are other activities I do not like. Peter, you are looking into strange activities as well, and I don't think I am of any help."

"Let me be real specific, Jacob. Yesterday, three men came through here. They arrived from Chicago at about ten in the morning. They went to town and had a quick lunch meeting. They left on the three pm Goodrich boat back to Chicago."

"Yes, that young Gates boy picked them up in that fancy carriage. Marvin comes out here often, so we kind of know each other. Yesterday, they had to stop and wait for the float to close, and they did not seem to like any inconvenience. One of the men yelled something, I guess at me, as they passed. He shook his fist, but I could not understand a word, so I just smiled and waved back."

Peter chuckled. "I appreciate your easygoing attitude. I tend to be far more likely to yell back something."

Jacob relit his pipe, but it was not lighting, so he tamped it out on his hand. "Something tells me you want to know if I recognized any of those three men." He looked at Peter, and Peter affirmed his notion. "That is one of the activities out here that concerns me. Those men, or at least two of them, have been through here before. In fact, they were here last week on Monday." Jacob was curious as Peter looked at the two papers he removed from his jacket.

A small smile came over Peter's face. "I thought so." He folded the papers and turned to Jacob. "You are very observant and very wise to stay out of their way. They have been involved in some dangerous activities here and in other cities. But now, I need to relax a bit. I see the steamer returning, so I bet you have work to do."

Jacob rose, shook Peter's hand, and moved quickly out to the gates. Peter had counted fifteen wagons and four buggies that had crossed the bridge during their chat. He also noticed his new traveling friend, Mr. Sam, sitting at the gate on the other side of the bridge. His timing was perfect. It was time to return before dark. Curiously, he noticed there was a lady in the buggy with him. *Umm, I don't think Sam would pick up a girlfriend,* he thought to himself.

Soon Sam pulled up to the north end of the bridge where Jacob and Peter were waiting. Jacob came around to let the passenger out, with an obvious look of pleasure.

"Peter, this is my beautiful wife, Ma-wish-ing-ga, but most call her Star, my shining star. Don't you agree?"

"It is such a pleasure to meet you." Peter took her hand and bowed slightly. She looked at him shyly with her deep, dark Native American eyes. She quickly looked away.

"I remember Mr. Sam told us you were his niece. I do not know how long I will be in the area, but I am sure it would be a great idea to get us all together with Miss Driscoll for a visit and a meal."

Jacob matched the invitation with one of his own. "With spring in the air, maybe you could all venture out here to the country for a picnic. You could use some fresh air I am sure."

Everyone smiled and agreed to follow up on this offer. Mr. Sam and Peter got into the buggy. Star stayed with Jacob and would return home with him as the day was ending soon. Peter thanked Jacob for his honest answers. Everyone hoped they would reconnect soon. Peter settled into his seat and quickly became settled into his thoughts as well. The ride was refreshing as they climbed from the lake, up through the tree-lined trail back toward the city. Because of the vacationer development along the lake area, many of the big hardwoods had been spared from the axe. It gave a dark, contemplative mood to their travel.

After nearly an hour of travel, Mr. Sam finally broke the silence. "Well, how it go?"

Peter had been making some notes and thinking a lot. He smiled and returned his pen and paper to his jacket pocket. Letting out a deep breath and stretching his arms over his head, he rubbed his injured arm nervously.

"I think I should come here on vacation sometime so that I could just enjoy this place more. Beauty seems to jump out at every turn. But I miss those sites that are in plain view when I am so involved in looking for things I cannot see clearly."

"Yes, you come back more, I think." Mr. Sam smiled.

Both were quiet. After a long pause, Sam added, "I think Miss Addy would like that."

Peter snapped a look at Mr. Sam, who had a mysterious smile on his face. They rode on home, both thinking of possibilities that lie ahead.

Chapter 13

Year 2000

After quickly cleaning up the cups and the cookie crumbs and putting away the thermos, I paused in the living room, admiring the oak work. I rubbed my hand around the fireplace mantel. I surveyed the entry again and was reminded to share some thoughts about the front door. I called to Meg.

"Meg, do you think you'll reinstall the door ringer in this old door?"

"What is a ringer? You mean a doorbell?"

"Well, yes and no. Remember, this is preelectricity, so it couldn't have been a doorbell as we know it today."

"Oh, yes. So, what kind of bell did they use? Was it one on the outside where you ring the clapper by shaking a cord?"

"Those were used, but this door had a different type. See this hole in the middle of the door panel. Some previous owner had it filled in. I expect the bell was a manual bell with the twist handle on the outside. The shaft went through the door and turned a clapper on a bell on the inside. They have some great examples of door ringers over at the history museum. In fact, these bells became quite a status symbol. Some were very elaborate. An ornamental blacksmith could probably make you an appropriate one today."

"I have seen fancy door knockers, but they would have been up higher and this hole is near the middle of the door."

"That's it exactly. Doorknockers seem to have been more of a European thing. But I'd have to do some research to clarify that. But you're right! Doorknockers were at about eye level, and these were mounted lower. They were very loud, much louder than their electric replacements. I think that was so a servant or maid could hear it from anywhere in the house."

"I'll try to find what you called an ornamental blacksmith in one of my restoration catalogues. They show a lot of replicas to replace antique, fancy metal pieces like pulls, knobs, foot scrapers, and such. That's a great idea to restore the door ringer."

"You'd have to be careful because people might want to borrow your door."

"What? Borrow my door?"

"A friend of mine here in town had an old home not far from here, and his door had a beautiful ringer in it. In fact, it was about the only interesting thing in that poor old house. He told me how several stage-production groups had borrowed his door with the ringer for an authentic prop in plays. I've always wondered how he filled in the door space when he lent it out."

Talking about the door and standing near the fireplace mantel reminded me of a question I wanted to ask. "Meg, you mentioned something about a curious place in the lathe work someplace down here. What were you talking about?"

"Oh, yes, thank you for reminding me. Let me show you. It's over here on the dining room side of this wall."

We came through the living room past the ornate oak fireplace mantel and around the corner on the dining room side of the fireplace. Meg stopped. "Remember how you said that it was the front entrance that attracted you to this house? Here's what captivated me. Just look at these pocket doors." She pulled the one out from the left side. "Isn't it gorgeous? And it still moves so easily."

"Are they both here?"

"Oh, yes." She pulled the right side one out by grasping the hidden latch on the edge of the door. "And notice the exquisite hardware." We both admired the ornate handcrafted hammered metal of not only the pull but also the finger holder. "Even the keyway was the same heavy hammered brass. So exact, so ornate. I do admire craftsmen." Meg tenderly touched the beautiful doors and audibly sighed.

"But the focus of my curiosity is over here in this wall. This is the same wall that contains the pocket door. Look at this very exact square hole in the lathe. What do you think this is all about?"

"I would say it would be a great place to hide something."

"You mean like a wall safe? That's what I was thinking."

"That's a possibility. Fancier homes of business-people might well have had safes or hidden storage places. Security was kind of odd back then, and many persons dealt with a great deal of cash, so it might fit. I am curious that this spot backs up to the corner fireplace in the living room. Maybe it connected to something there?"

"Now you are imagining a spooky story where you lean against the mantel and a secret door opens up."

"Oh, did you and Scooby Doo find a secret door?"

"No, you can see what I found—a hole in my wall."

"Yes, but notice one more thing." We moved around back into the living room area in front of the fireplace. "See, there are a couple of pieces of this mantel missing. There appears to have been some posts or columns, one on each side. And remember, just on the other side of this wall is the closet with the hidden door that went into the owner's study or den area."

"Do you think this could have been some connector to secretly open that door? And a place to hide the mechanism, or secret papers, or money, or—?"

"Whoa. Now you're starting to mind-race and imagine like I do."

"Yes. I guess I've been around you too long. It must be catching. Speaking of catching, did I tell you about the dog?"

"Yes, you mentioned that your dog didn't seem to like this house at the beginning."

"No, not my dog, the ghost dog!"

I was moving toward the rear door to head outside, and I snapped to attention to look at Meg. I could see she had a very serious, almost scared, look on her face, not the usually nonchalant grin and smirk. I'm sure my eyes squinted and my forehead wrinkled like a question. Before I could ask anything, Meg spoke.

"Yes, there was a ghost. My dog saw it, and my young niece saw it too."

"Really? Tell me more, like when, how, where?" Questions were swirling in my brain and streaming out of my mouth.

Meg took a deep breath and told me her story.

"Yes, my dog wouldn't walk through this house with me at first. She would sit by the rear door and kind of growl, looking straight ahead, her head on her paws. That was very strange behavior because she has always gone with me to many houses. It kind of unnerved me, but my husband laughed it off, and we went on to work on this house. About a week into it, while we were still in the tearing off the plaster stage, my niece came over to help us work. She was standing in the old dining room leaning against a ladder, when suddenly something hit the ladder hard, rocking it and scaring her."

"Go on, go on please. This explains another curiosity I haven't even shared with you yet because I couldn't make it fit."

"OK. I'll finish my story, and then you can fill me in with what you know. Anyway, a couple days later, she and I were in the same room working over in that corner." Meg motioned to the corner opposite the opening to the living room. "Suddenly, we both sensed something at the same time and turned toward the living room. I recall I'd detected a motion out of the corner of my eye and thought my husband had arrived to help. I didn't notice, but my niece had sensed the same motion. There in the doorway, for just an instant, I saw a dog. It was dark, maybe curly fur, and it was growling. Then it was gone. It was just there for an instant. But we both saw it."

Meg paused and looked at me. "You're smiling. You don't believe me, do you?"

"No, no. Au contraire, my friend!" I exclaimed. "I believe it. I not only believe it, but this is the evidence that helps more pieces fit together. Go on, please."

"Well, I was spooked, so I asked a pastor friend, Paul Newell, to come in and bless the house."

"You did that believing the haunt would leave. Correct?"

"Yes."

"And did it work?"

"Well, kind of. We didn't see the dog again. But two weeks later, my friend Ann from Whitehall came over, and she brought her dog. The dog was a bit nervous but nothing more than normal for a new setting. I was showing them around, first downstairs and then upstairs. When we stepped into the upstairs hall, the dog barked furiously and her hair stood straight up on her back. My friend spoke sharply to her, but she ran down the hall to the back room and barked again. We went down the hall, where she was standing by the balcony door. When I opened it, she ran out onto the open balcony and jumped off."

"Oh my. Was she hurt? Did she survive?"

"Yes, fortunately she landed on a pile of trash and that probably helped. But it ended up she did break her front leg."

"So what happened then?"

"I called Rev. Newell back, and he blessed the house again. Since then the spirit has left. We've had no unusual happenings with our dogs or us. What are you thinking? Weird, huh?"

"Strange, certainly, but I've long ago given up any claim to insight on truth or real or any of that. Still you'd better hold on to your hat, because I think I can fit this puzzle piece in. Are you ready?"

Meg just stared at me and nodded her head.

"I think I have a picture of the dog, and by the way, his name is Wally."

Chapter 14

Year 1891

Alex had gone to the mill early to finish some payroll records and invoices. He had just completed addressing the last invoice. He was sending it to the Chicago Lumber Exchange in payment for two loads of lumber. The lumber had been shipped by schooner and would arrive sometime on Sunday. He was startled from his work when Malcolm, one of the mill workers, came running into the office, breathless. "Alex, ya must pull the whistle, lad! Pull the whistle! It's really bad!"

"Malcolm, calm down. What are you babbling about?"

"The fire, lad. The fire! It's spreading fast!"

"What? Where?" Alex stammered.

"Up on Pine Street. The whistle, lad! Now!" And Malcolm ran out, leaving the door open. With the door ajar, Alex smelled the smoke immediately. He ran outside and looked south; he could only see smoke and flames. Fire bells pierced the air. The steam whistle from the Torrent Mill next door went off. Alex jumped into high speed. He ran to the mill's steam engine shed, where he met Sammy Johnson, the assistant steam-room operator. "Pull the whistle, Sammy!"

Sammy stuttered, and he spoke with a lisp and stammer, especially when excited. "I-I-I'm-m-m only sus-sus-p-p-posed—"

"Sammy, I'll take the responsibility. Pull the whistle!" As the whistle blew, the whistle at the Ryerson Mill down along the lake to the west also blew. Smoke was spreading over the entire town, and Alex began to cough and choke. He pulled out his handkerchief and held it over his nose.

Whistles and fire bells demanded attention. Some people seemed dazed and just wandered around. Other people were frantic, with teams and wagons being pushed and pulled in haste up and down the streets. Every lumber town had seen fires before. Piles and piles of wood and sawdust are a fire waiting to happen. Alex assumed one of the mills was burning. Yet being responsible as he was, he put away his work before he left the office. As he rushed up toward Clay Street, a worried lump formed in his throat.

First, what he had assumed about this being a mill fire was certainly wrong. Not only was it not a mill fire, but a strong wind from the north had also masked the true enormity of the danger. As he approached, he could see some buildings had already collapsed while others were completely engulfed. Reaching the hill, he could see that city hall at Clay and Jefferson was well in flames. Just then a gust of wind tore a bunch of shingles from the tall clock tower of city hall. People shouted and pointed south as the flaming missiles landed on top of another home further down Pine Street.

"Oh, no!" Alex gasped, and he feared the worst. What about Priscilla? The Wallaces' house was surely in grave danger. The heat was intense. Suddenly there came a loud roar. He looked around just as the roof and clock tower of city hall caved in, creating a shower of hot ashes and cinders that the wind quickly carried southward.

Wondering what had happened to the fire-fighting equipment, Alex noticed one fire engine company yelling and motioning wildly. He would later find out that the highly touted water station had failed. There was not enough water pressure to fight the blaze. The pumpers stood helpless and useless. The long city council debates over funds to build an adequate water system no longer mattered.

Old tried and true methods were set up instantly. Lines and lines of mill hands passed buckets. People soaked burlap gunnysacks and pounded out the falling cinders as soon as they landed. Many teamsters worked to quiet their teams of horses, terrified by the fire, so water tanks could be hauled from the lake or personal belongings could be rescued from *individual homes*.

Priscilla and Mrs. Wallace must have lost everything. Alex sighed. In the midst of the fury, he momentarily remembered the two wagons he had seen loaded with the Wallaces' furniture. But there was no time to consider what that might have meant. Not now.

"Come here, Alex!" He suddenly saw Peter coming toward him. "I need your help. Take these clothes to a safe place. They are from Addy's house."

"What is happening? What about Miss Driscoll? What about Priscilla and Mrs. Wallace?"

Quickly turning to go, Peter cut him off short. "It's bad, Alex. I'm afraid both homes are burned to the ground."

Although the wind subsided at midday, giving all some hope of saving structures, in the afternoon the wind, with a mind of its own, shifted directly and blew from the south. That caused a mess, for the fire moved back over houses and buildings that were already burning. The people fighting the existing fires were forced back as existing structures were rekindled and fanned alive by the hot south wind. The fire burned clear back to Muskegon Lake, but not before terrible destruction and damage had been wrought. By dark, 250 homes and businesses were damaged or destroyed. Hundreds of people were homeless, so churches were hurriedly opening doors and gathering resources to help those who were most desperate.

When the wind changed, Alex knew the mill was now threatened. He and the steam-room worker, Sammy Johnson, had miraculously found a cart to use and saved most of the files and records. They and another mill hand had pushed the cart two blocks to the west and stored the material in one of the vacant sheds behind an office building Mr. Wallace owned. That area escaped the blaze. The last item they moved was Alex's oak desk. They escaped the area just as the roof of the main mill building blew over onto the smaller office building. Everything else was lost. The three men finally rested on the higher ground, exhausted from their efforts. They stopped, gasping for breath, and watched their beloved, and often hated, mill as it was reduced to a pile of smoking, smoldering timber.

The south winds had pushed the fire clear through the Wallace and Smithson Mill. There was much to burn at the mill; not only piles and piles of cut lumber but piles and piles of slab wood lined both sides of the mill property. Much of it was dry, and it went up like a match. The mill workers rushed in a futile effort to save the mill office and sawyer building. There is really only one big important piece of equipment at a mill and that is the saw and carriage system. All of that was lost, and the finality was a shock.

The mill hands and other volunteers carried hundreds of water buckets from the nearby lake. Before the fire, the workmen had always kept the many roof barrels full, but those alone were not enough. Nothing could stop that wind. It pushed harder on the flames than the water could push back. In the great race, people eventually realized, as evidenced on every soot-spattered face, the flames would win.

It was late when Alex finally found Priscilla and Mrs. Wallace. Mrs. Wallace had ordered tents and tables set up and food prepared. In the tragedy, she was not mindful of her own loss but was helping those who had been scared, displaced, and devastated by the fire. Several nurse friends assisted Mrs. Wallace and treated many injured folk. Many persons sat in a paralyzed daze on the ground with a simple cup of tea or coffee or soup for comfort. The city was in shock, yet many persons like Mrs. Wallace and Miss Driscoll had organized quickly and rushed in to help. How could she and Priscilla even begin to react to the complete loss of their home?

Alex found Peter much later that night, when panic had given way to a mild stunned silence. Peter was trying to help Addy find a place to rest, fearing that if she did not rest soon, she would surely faint from exhaustion. Peter reported seeing Priscilla and Mrs. Wallace entering the Occidental Hotel, where Mr. Wallace had secured a suite for them.

Peter was stern and deep in thought when Alex asked, "What do you think happened, Peter?"

Peter did not speak, but his frustration showed by the movement of his jaw quietly grinding his teeth. Alex was worried, for Peter seemed as tense as a bent black-willow bow, about to snap at any minute. After several minutes, Alex spoke again, but with a different question. "Are you all right, Peter?" Again there was no reply.

Slowly Peter turned toward the lake. He stared at the charred and smoking mess. He swept his arm across the sad view, sighed deeply, and tried to speak. When he did, his voice was hoarse from having breathed too much smoke all day. He took another drink from the cup he held, cleared some soot from his throat, and spit on the ground.

"That mill over yonder there was the only target of this mess. All this other destruction, Addy's home, your Priscilla's house, was just not necessary. As always, when big money speaks, it's the little people who get hurt. It sure rings true this time." He spat on the ground again, appropriately punctuating his angry statement.

Alex answered, "Peter, can you prove any of what you are saying?"

"I'll surely try. But I doubt it. A sawmill fire is about as accidental a happening as could occur. However, the fire marshal has already suggested the fire started in a barn behind a rooming house near Clay and Pine. These guys aren't too original it seems."

"What do you mean by that?" Alex asked.

"Oh, nothing. I guess I was just thinking of the fire that got me started in this business back in Chicago twenty years ago. Do you remember? No, I suppose not, for you were very young. Well, most reports were that the fire was started by a cow kicking over a lantern in a barn."

"Yes, I do remember learning that. I get your point," Alex said.

"Go get some rest, Alex, but check with me tomorrow afternoon, for I might need your help. I think we all better go give prayers of thanks at St. Mary's tomorrow. I'll come find you around two."

With that, Peter nodded good-bye, added nothing more, and moved off toward the mill and the corner of Pine and Clay. His limp seemed quite pronounced.

"I hope you get some rest too, Peter," Alex called. Peter did not acknowledge him but limped away with his head down.

Chapter 15

Year 2000

Meg turned toward me with a jerk. I thought she was going to choke me or maybe something worse. "You what? You have a picture? I mean, how? Wally? How do you know that? This is impossible. Hurry and fill me in."

"Hold on. Hold on. Not so fast. Everything will be clear in its own time. It took over one hundred years to get this far; a little longer won't hurt a thing, except maybe your curiosity."

"Yeah, you know me. Patience is not in my vocabulary. You better let me in on your little secret right now."

"Well, let's start back at the fire. You have heard and read about the Pine Street Fire of 1891. This whole story, this house, and the dog are all connected to that fire."

"Yes, you've commented before that this house was probably burned because of where it originally sat over on Pine Street. But why didn't I find any evidence of the burn? No charring, no burn marks—nothing."

"Let me explain. If you look at the path of the fire as described in that library reference I showed you, this house would have been burned not once but twice."

"Twice?"

"Well, sort of. The fire was pushed south from its start near Clay and Webster and surely would have ignited your house on its original lot. With its dry pine construction, it would not take long for the house to be engulfed in the inferno. The fire burned south for several blocks to the vicinity of Irwin Street over near Evergreen Cemetery. Then the oddest thing happened. The wind changed one hundred and eighty degrees and pushed the fire straight back north over the same area it had already burned. Therefore, in all likelihood, this house burned twice. As the conspiracy would claim, the fire then went on north to burn the intended arson targets, the two mills at the edge of Lake Muskegon."

"But how does this house exist today? I thought we have been discussing all the ways it was built befitting the style of the Lumber Era before the fire?"

"Well, you're right. I believe it was burned completely and rebuilt with very few changes, probably by someone very close to the owner or the owner's family. There were some notable deletions from the earlier period, such as no stable building out back. There were also notable additions. You showed me evidence of central heating being installed and most likely, electric lights. Your date on that central heating boot is close to matching the arrival of electricity to the city. This house would probably have been one of the first updated for electric lights. Muskegon has some historical significance in the development of useful electricity; you might like to read up on that later.

"But we want to discuss this house specifically. Remember, this was an upscale home, and those would have been very upscale additions at the turn of the century. Also remember that probably only the more affluent families would have had the money, either from savings or insurance, to rebuild their homes so quickly after a devastating fire. I think some of the other changes just occurred over time. Originally after the fire, your house would have been built with summer porches that may not have disappeared until the 1950s or '60s. It is hard to place the order of change without the original plans."

We both paused and moved to sit on a makeshift bench made of a board and two sawhorses. I continued explaining to Meg.

"The stair outline your carpenters discovered on the rear wall suggests the summer porch was probably removed because of deterioration, not because of lack of necessity or usefulness. Many of the other porches like it around town were incorporated into the building structure, had good roofs added, and were closed in. These changes made them part of the structure more than just an appendage. The ones on this house may have been more attachments and were therefore doomed to easier deterioration. Remember, your side porch had been closed in more like a room. You had it removed when you moved the house because it was just an attachment and had rotted anyway."

"OK," Meg finally interrupted. "I understand about the house. Now, Mr. Sherlock Holmes, get to the point. What about the dog?"

"Sorry to prolong this story, but until you reported your events with the haunting, I had not been able to put into words events that happened to me here. I had three or four events actually. When I first arrived at this house to change the locks, I distinctly recall having a strange feeling. You know I've told you before how I felt instantly attached to this house. I sometimes joked, 'This house has a story to tell.' Remember that? Well, when I opened the door the first time, I felt a current of air or a rush of something go past me, like exhaling after holding your breath for a long time. At the time, I shrugged it off.

"The second event occurred as I explored the house. It may have been on that first day or when I came back later to finish the job. I was alone, as usual. I went upstairs and as you know, found very little. Back in that far left room, the previous owner had tried to set up a small kitchen for his upstairs apartment. He had literally nailed the upper shelf section of an old Michigan Baker cabinet to the wall for the kitchen cabinets. Do you know what I mean by a Michigan Baker?"

"Oh, yes. I often see those kinds of cabinets at auctions or old farm sales. It would be one with the flour bin and sifter in one corner, wouldn't it? It also usually has an enameled work surface that pulls out to create a perfect surface to roll dough or maybe cool baked goods. But go on, somehow I bet this is going to tie into our story."

"Yes, but I'll come back to that. I didn't find anything upstairs except that cabinet and made a note to retrieve it later. On the main floor there was nothing, so I proceeded down to the basement. I have joked many times about finding a dead body in one of these old houses, and my wife frets I'll be attacked and killed one day in some musty basement when I wander in these old houses alone. As you remember, the basement here had few windows and was particularly dark, dank, and dreary. My flashlight was never very bright, so it was of little help.

"You'll also remember the basement was mostly an open space except for the one room in the rear corner. Now, I have helped repossess dozens of these houses over the years with equally dark and spooky basements, so this place was nothing unusual. But somehow I still expected to find something. I can't explain it, but I expected to find an animal, some critter. The basement window's glass was broken, so I thought I'd be surprised by a stray cat or worse, maybe a raccoon. The sense of an animal presence got stronger as I entered that rear room. It was just a strong feeling; I can't explain it any other way. But I found no critters, no surprises, only strange feelings, dust, and cobwebs. I shrugged it off and went on with my work.

"The third event gets back to that upstairs cupboard. Oh, by the way, I did find the base cabinet downstairs, although it had been used as a workbench and had been somewhat abused. But like you, I respect old antique pieces, so I took both sections home. The odd thing is that now, three years later, I still have that cabinet for some reason."

Meg interrupted, "You know why. You kept them because they are a part of the story of this house. They must be; everything fits together. Go on."

"Back to the cabinet I took off the wall upstairs. There is one more detail I've not told you. When I took the cabinet down from the wall, there was an old picture stashed or hidden on the very top. An old picture, not framed, quite beaten, stained, and pretty cruddy actually."

"A picture of the house, I am guessing?"

"No, not the house. What else fits into our story?"

"Oh my, the dog. It couldn't be. You found a picture of the dog."

Chapter 16

Year 1891

The events of the next few days confused everyone. Mostly people worried about helping each other, in spite of their individual losses and problems. In the small town of Muskegon, everyone knew people who were directly affected by the fire. Many people had lost everything and needed clothing as well as places to stay. Neighbors offered extra rooms in their homes to whole families just to help get them through this disastrous time. By midweek some sense of normalcy had returned to the city. Crews were already starting to remove the ruins of the destroyed houses. One larger building needed to have its brick walls collapsed and pulled down so no one would get hurt should they cave in. But mostly only ash and charred wood were left, mixed with many lost hopes and shattered dreams. Those had gone up in the smoke along with the houses.

Alex and Priscilla walked and talked. “Are you sure you want to do this, Priscilla?” Alex was convinced it was not a good idea at all. “I know you loved the house,” he went on, “but—”

Priscilla cut him off midsentence. “When my auntie would bring me to work with her, I felt at home, more so than I did in the apartment I shared with my own mother and brother. In many ways, right up until now, I can say, *I grew up there at that house.* That house is the only home I've ever known. Yes, I loved that house and I am very sad, but I will hold on to things I know are more important. I am thankful the fire did not take you away.” With that she pulled Alex close and hugged his arm as they walked on, passing through the surrounding debris toward what they both expected to be the very worst.

Alex looked over at Priscilla's face. Through her toughness and resolve, he noticed the tear that slowly streaked her cheek. He patted her arm in support, keeping his mouth shut, knowing it was enough to have the privilege of supporting Priscilla during this terrible time.

As they turned the corner onto Pine Street, they were met with an awful sight—burned buildings and devastation. Some small corners of wood framing stuck out from the ash; some cement block foundations stood taller than the rest. There were some chimneys standing here and there, but most of what had been familiar was simply gone. They only walked a short distance and stopped.

They both surveyed the mess. Priscilla let out a deep sigh. It may have come from her fear or from her resolve. Whichever it was, she took in a deep breath, squared her shoulders, and spoke.

"Thank you, Alex, for coming with me. I don't know why I came. I'm not really looking for anything. This is about how I knew it would look. Doesn't it make you feel, well, sad?" Priscilla seemed lost in her thoughts and far away.

Alex answered slowly. "Yes, it does make me sad, but more so angry and frustrated. You know Peter suspects foul play, but he has no proof. It is all circumstantial evidence. He's afraid the guilty will never be caught."

"Oh, Alex, it's all so dreadful. Let's go back now, for I know Mrs. Wallace needs my help. She is moving, you know. She has asked me to come with her to Chicago!"

Alex broke away and stood facing Priscilla. "You are going away? That is too much tragedy for me to take. I lost my job and the mill. My friend Peter has already departed. And now you tell me you are leaving with the Wallaces and moving to Chicago or wherever?"

Priscilla looked him straight in the eye and placed her hands gently on his arms. "Alex, do not fret, for nothing has happened yet. It is all just talk. Now, you know I care deeply about you. I do not want to add to your already burdensome load. Do not worry now, for we are together. You have been such a dear for supporting me so. No. Let's return to the hotel. We can talk about upcoming plans later when they are more certain."

As they turned the corner at the Muskegon Bank, one block up from the hotel, Addy Driscoll was coming out of the main entrance. Alex and Priscilla were shocked to see Peter holding the door for her.

"Peter!" Alex exclaimed. "I thought you had been called back to Chicago." Alex excitedly pumped Peter's hand in relief.

"Well, I am afraid not, my friend." Then, with a nearly undetectable glance to Addy, he added, "In fact, it is worse than that. I have lost my job and have been told not to return."

Peter stopped, looked down, and seemed at a loss for words. Priscilla and Alex exchanged puzzled looks. Addy spoke up to break the tense silence.

"Peter and I do have some news, and we feel, for now, it is good news. Let's go to the hotel, where we can talk more comfortably." All agreed and went with anticipation to the tea room of the Occidental Hotel, a short walk down the street.

When they were seated, the tea was ordered. Addy and Peter seemed to silently ask each other, "Who should start?" Peter spoke first.

"Addy hurriedly gathered all her papers to escape the fire. Alex, your wise actions of saving records of the mill have been of more value than just office records. Addy and I have been pouring over the mill records, as well as Addy's father's business dealings with Mr. Wallace. Together we are convinced there is enough evidence indicting Mr. Wallace and his business partners, both here and in Chicago, of treachery and malice. So as the owners of the Wallace and Smithson Mill have been confronted, they have made Miss Driscoll an unusual offer."

Alex interjected a question. "Peter, are you saying Mr. Wallace did not act alone, as it originally appeared?"

Peter clarified, "I believe it is a conspiracy involving numerous people. I can only hope the authorities will sort it all out and bring those guilty to justice."

"But," Addy added quickly, "getting back to the interesting offer Peter referred to, we have just gotten some delightful news. You both may have not known that my late father was involved in a sordid business deal with Mr. Wallace several years ago. My father believed Mr. Wallace was cheating him out of his money. My father had some pressing debts and asked Mr. Wallace for an advance on what was owed. He hurriedly signed some papers and took the small advance, assuming the rest would be forthcoming. Later, my father realized he had actually signed away his right to the rest of the money owed him. My father was furious and I believe deeply embarrassed at his error."

Addy paused, took a hanky from her sleeve, and daubed her eyes. Now it was Peter's turn to lay his hand on her arm for comfort, as Alex had done for Priscilla. Composing herself, she went on.

"Some people believe my father was so distraught he may have taken his own life. Others believe the stress simply caused his weak heart to give out. None of us can truly know the truth. However, Peter's suspicions led him to have a private conversation with Mr. Wallace and his lawyer, Mr. Hart."

Peter put up his hand and entered the conversation.

"Yes, I've had two private confrontations, I mean, conversations, with Mr. Wallace and Mr. Hart. I tried to point out the circumstantial evidence that implicates him and his partners. He didn't admit anything. However, I knew he was in a hurry to get out of town, so I pressed him to repay Miss Driscoll the money he should have paid her father."

Addy was excited and interrupted. "Peter has convinced your boss to unload the burden of property he owns in the city so he can leave town quickly."

Alex sat speechless. Priscilla took Alex's arm. "Yes, Alex, I have known of this possibility. Mrs. Wallace confided in me just last evening. But I feel so deeply for dear Mrs. Wallace. She feels such sorrow for all who have been harmed and feels helpless to do anything to assist." Her voice trailed off in sad reflection.

"Well," Peter continued, "I can't do much about any of that now. I have no authority since I've been terminated. But I have convinced your likely-to-be accused former boss to do at least one redeeming thing in his disgusting life."

Addy spoke up as she could see Peter's anger rising. Touching him gently, she added, "Peter has convinced Mr. Wallace to sign over all his land holdings here in Muskegon to me. I'm sure he and/or his associates were also connected to my father's death, a fact that has gone unproven. At the bank, I just completed signing the preliminary papers. Now they are to be approved by the lawyers and then properly recorded by the register of deeds. I hear the county offices are being set up in the basement of St. Mary's Church and at the Occidental Hotel Annex. We think the transaction will be finalized in less than a week."

Alex and Priscilla stared back and forth at each other with their mouths open, completely at a loss for words. "You mean..." Alex finally stammered. "You mean..."

Addy continued, "Alex, we are not yet sure what it means, but of this we are sure. Peter has promised to stay and help organize my new affairs. Would you be interested in a job as office manager and assistant to Mr. Frisk?"

"Would I? This is all too..." In all his excitement, he abandoned all decorum, and nearly tipping over the table, he gave Priscilla a hug.

"Be careful, Mr. Alex," she scolded, holding on to her hat and grinning from ear to ear. They all laughed together; it was the first good news they had shared since the terrible fire.

The rest of the week was a blur of intertwining events. Addy was busy trying to make plans and set up new housekeeping after the loss of both her father and their family home. Peter was setting up an office in her father's old building west of the mill site, on Western Avenue. There were couriers and lawyers coming and going in a steady stream. Priscilla talked to Mrs. Wallace, who told, or rather ordered, her husband to donate the furniture Alex had rescued from the mill office to Addy and Peter. He was more than happy to get rid of it so he didn't have to deal with it. His only interest was in getting out of town and making business and housing arrangements in Chicago as soon as possible. Alex was pleased because with Mr. Wallace's donation, he got his old desk back to use in the new office.

Mr. Wallace quickly left for Chicago, leaving his wife and Priscilla to clean up things in Muskegon. While they were alone in the hotel suite one day, Mrs. Wallace asked Priscilla to bring a pot of tea with two cups and sit with her by the window. When Priscilla came into the sitting room, she noticed Mrs. Wallace looking out the window wistfully, gazing south down Webster Avenue. “Pardon me, ma’am.” Priscilla feared she was interrupting her friend’s thoughts or maybe her grief.

“Oh, do come sit near me, dear.” The gracious Mrs. Wallace directed Priscilla to the other chair set in front of the window. Priscilla poured the tea for Mrs. Wallace and herself and then sat feeling warm and comfortable with her close friend, who was also her boss.

Mrs. Wallace went on, “Priscilla, you know how important you have been and are to me. I can never forget your devotion and care. However, I must move on, for better or worse, and I do not know to what or where. I can’t ask you to follow when I don’t even know where we’re heading.”

“But Mrs.—”

She lifted her hand and cut Priscilla off. “I have already talked to your friend Addy. She would be delighted and consider it a privilege if you would come to work for her and help her to arrange her new home and furnishings. What do you think?"

Priscilla just sat in stunned silence, hardly sipping her tea and nervously fingering her cup.

Enjoying the flavorful tea herself, Mrs. Wallace said, "My dear, you had better take a drink before the tea is cold. Maybe it will help. It seems the cat's got your tongue." Then she smiled. Her eyes twinkled keenly, and she laughed out loud.

Priscilla was drawn out of her stunned, silent confusion. She sipped her tea without tasting it and said, "Thank you, ma'am! Thank you very much!"

~

After church the next Sunday, Priscilla asked Alex to walk with her over to Pine Street. As they walked, they filled each other in on all the events of the previous week.

"You do realize, don't you," Alex began, "that your new boss, Mrs. Driscoll, owns the spot where your old house was burned?"

"Yes, I am aware of that. I have no idea, or I'm sure, does she, what to do about any of this. She and Peter will figure it out in due time."

As they walked up Pine Street and neared the site of the burned-out house, not much had changed since their first visit. Some workers had pulled down the chimney, and someone had kicked loose some bricks and started a pile in the rear toward a charred tree that had been near the now-nonexistent stable.

"Oh my," was the chorused sigh as they both exhaled audibly. They poked around in the sooty mess and kept their thoughts to themselves.

Finally, Priscilla asked, "Have you seen Phillip around town lately?"

"Oh, yes, and the last time, I saw him, he was driving one of Geordie's livery wagons. Geordie hired him to drive, and they have been busy from dawn to dark with the teams and wagons helping people clean up, move on, or rebuild. 'Lots and lots of work,' he said. In fact, when I saw him, he was so proud. Do you remember that tall, regal team of black geldings your Mr. Wallace had? Remember when they came charging past us that day just before the fire?"

"I remember," Priscilla answered. "They were being driven and whipped by that mean man who used to work at the mill."

"That's the one. Pattone was his name, and I haven't seen him around town since the fire. All the horses used at the mill were kept at the livery. All except Mr. Wallace's personal buggy horse that he kept at home. What was its name? I forgot."

Priscilla spoke up, "I believe Phillip called her Star because of the marking on her forehead."

Alex continued. "The mill's best horses were a matched team of black geldings. After the fire, the mill's directors made a quick deal with Geordie, and now he owns all the mill's teams. Geordie has given Phillip responsibility to work with the black team to calm them down and reassure them after their abusive treatment. Phillip has obviously been spending extra time with the team, for they now look shiny and sleek and prance proudly, as their regal heritage prescribes. Phillip is in his glory, and Geordie speaks high praise for his exceptional work."

Priscilla laughed as Alex imitated Geordie's Scottish accent with a hearty, "Ya, he's a mighty good lad, that Phillip boy."

Alex and Priscilla both enjoyed the comic relief because otherwise the scene was bleak and depressing. Alex picked up a stick and began to poke in the ashes. Priscilla stayed out of the mess and walked around to the back of the house near the old, demolished stable.

"I wonder what happened to that dog, Wally?" she mumbled, mostly to herself. "Mr. Wallace and Phillip were the only ones he liked much. Mr. Wallace would sneak him into his office sometimes; that's as tender as I ever say Mr. Wallace was when he petted Wally. Surely he would have run away from the fire. I have to hope someone would welcome his good company and give him a new home."

Alex was poking around the pile of ashes and pieces of charred lumber near where the chimney bricks had been pulled down. His stick hit one particular piece of wood that seemed less destroyed than the others. Struck by this oddity, he pried it up and noticed it was oak. Alex knew oak burned much more slowly than the pine used in construction. *This piece seemed to be a door or part of a door frame, or... No, I bet it was the mantel of the fireplace,* he thought to himself.

Priscilla heard Alex yelling, "Priscilla, come here." He was excited and came rushing from the pile of char and ashes, holding something. It appeared to be some kind of box.

"What is it, Alex?" she inquired.

Breathlessly, he reported. "I was poking around over near where they pulled down the chimney. Do you know anything about something hidden or a secret hiding place anywhere near or around the fireplace?"

"Heavens, no. Why, I've cleaned every inch of that fireplace for years. I polished that mantel piece especially well, for Mrs. Wallace had special crystal candleholders she displayed there. What are you talking about?"

"This box," he explained as he held it out to her.

It was dirty, as were his hands, and she shuddered away. "Get that away from me. It's filthy."

"Let me set it on this pile of bricks for a minute."

As he set it down, he thumped it to get the ash and soot off of the surface. As he did that, the small clasp lock, having been compromised by the heat, simply fell off. Alex opened the metal box, albeit with some difficulty. They both anxiously peered at the meager contents. Inside, there were a few papers folded, one in an envelope, maybe three or four sheets total. Because it was a metal box, it must have gotten pretty hot, but it probably had been partially protected by both the chimney and the oak mantel. Could it have been in some secret safe or hiding place in or near the fireplace mantel? Why hadn't it have been removed with the rest of the household items? Possibilities swirled in their minds. It must have been forgotten or overlooked in the haste of packing things from the house and readying for the move out of town. The edges of the papers were crisp—dried from the heat but not charred. Alex carefully opened the top one and gasped.

"What is it?" Priscilla asked as she moved around the brick pile to get a closer look.

"It appears to be a legal paper, possibly a deed," Alex said as he examined it quickly. "I must get this to Peter immediately. Do excuse me, but I must."

With that, he ran off toward downtown, leaving the bewildered Priscilla standing among the charred remains of her former life.

~

"Alex, you would make a grand investigator," Peter acknowledged as he studied the paper, which had been hastily thrust at him. Alex stood by, winded and puffing. "This could be it," Peter mumbled, quickly grabbing his jacket and putting it on as they both rushed out the office door.

"Alex, I must get this information to the authorities, especially to my old bosses in Chicago. Please apologize to Addie and Priscilla for my quick departure. I must get to Chicago. I will be in touch by wire as soon as I know or learn something. By the way, where is Priscilla? I thought you said you were both at the Pine Street house?"

"Oh, my," Alex gasped. "I just ran off and left her there."

So the two men rushed in opposite directions, calling, "I'll be in touch soon," over their shoulders as they hurried away. Alex found Priscilla about halfway back to the Pine Street site.

"You left me standing in that mess! You had better have some really good reason, Alex, or I'm never going to forgive you." She wagged her finger as she spoke. Fortunately, young Alex was smart enough to pay close attention when a woman, especially one with a scowl on her face, wagged her finger at him. He quickly and sincerely apologized.

"Oh my dear, I am so sorry, but this is the news we needed. As we speak, Peter is in the process of contacting the authorities both here and in Chicago. We may have found the proverbial missing link to tie a knot of guilt around the necks of that Mr. Wallace of yours and his business partners."

"Alex, please don't speak so harshly and vindictively. I have dreadful fears as to what may happen to my dear friend Mrs. Wallace."

"Don't worry! Nothing implicates her in any way or drags her into this mess. She was happily not included in her husband's shady business dealings."

"Thank you for that reassurance. Now, tell me clearly what this paper you just found was and what it has to do with this fire mess!"

"Priscilla, it is the deed to the rooming house and stable where everyone agrees the fire was set. This is a direct link to the man from Chicago, Mr. Johansson, who we have suspected all along of being behind the whole plot. Peter thinks that because of this deed and the location of the fire, there is finally enough concrete evidence. Now the police and other authorities can bring charges and prosecute. I just wish there was some way we could directly connect Mr. Johansson to Mr. Wallace."

Priscilla grabbed Alex's sleeve, "But there is. Mrs. Wallace told me a story once of how she came to own a beautiful set of tea cups. She and Mr. Wallace went with Mr. and Mrs. Johansson on a business trip to Toronto. Mr. Johansson gave them to the Wallaces to celebrate their successful business plans. That would surely connect them, wouldn't it, Alex?"

"Priscilla, you are amazing. Peter will be glad to trace down your report of that meeting. Hopefully we will all have lots to be thankful for very soon.

~

The days of summer arrived, lifting everyone's spirits out of and past the recent tragedy. Other mills were still running, working on last winter's supply of logs that had been boomed along the river. Some felt a certain caution, for they knew the supply of wood could not last. There was enough for this year, but next? What was next for the area after the pines were gone? No one knew, but many wondered.

Other industries related to wood production had already been established. There were several big shingle mills, especially up on Sanford's Bayou. More interesting yet was the news of a business taking over one of the old mill buildings out toward Lakeside. That company was gearing up to make rollers for window shades. There had also been a rise of veneer mills that produced thin pieces of wood sought after by furniture manufacturers. There was even speculation that furniture companies themselves would come to Muskegon. With all the expertise and labor available there to handle wood and wood products, Muskegon seemed destined to grow.

But the sudden departure of one of the biggest mill companies, the "accidental" burning of several other mills, and the constant rumors of other mills in danger of closing left plenty of room for worry in people's minds. Talk and rumors were constant. Businessmen chatted at the Century Club over cigars and drinks. Similarly, a group of ladies met in Mrs. Sanford's backyard. Miss Driscoll helped host the party and led the discussion about some of the forthcoming business projects. Mill workers and laborers throughout the town busied themselves gossiping about the latest possibilities.

The warmth of summer, the bloom of the peonies and daisies, and the cool breezes off the lake reminded folks that Muskegon was a wonderful place to live.

It was on one such warm day in late June that Addy Driscoll came into Alex's office holding a telegram in her hand. Alex rose, greeted her promptly, and commented, "You look very chipper this morning, ma'am."

"Thank you, dear Alex. I am very pleased today, for this is a wire from Peter. He may be moving back to Muskegon soon."

"That is great news. Peter has wired here regularly and kept me busy getting deeds and records organized. He has had me running all over town. Some papers I've had to send back to him; some have gone to one of several lawyers here in town. Then I go back to pick them up and file them or get them to the register of deeds or back to him. He is surely the most organized man I've ever known." Alex and Addy laughed at his fake frustration.

Alex became reflective and commented, "I do miss—dare I say—his friendship. Though he is nearly old enough to be my father, he has been a dear friend." At that, Alex paused quietly and recalled the few images he had of his father, who had died in a logging accident many years before. But he shook his head, as if to brush away the cobwebs and foggy memories that had suddenly clouded his conversation with Addy.

"I am sure he misses you also, Alex. He often comments on how thankful he is for your able help. He has great hope for your successful future in business. Have you ever considered becoming a lawyer?"

"Oh no, ma'am. I'd never have the resources to undertake such a profession as that. No, I am glad to be helpful to Peter, for he has taught me so much about investigation and the insurance business in general. But ma'am, what else does Peter say? What is this about him moving back here to Muskegon?"

"Yes, I nearly forgot the best news. Well, after Peter presented his bosses at the Chicago Fire Insurance Company with the evidence you uncovered, they, of course, gave him his job back. Peter says that further investigations have uncovered a similar 'accidental fire' at a mill near Manistee, which just happened to be owned by a Chicago man who was Mr. Wallace's business partner. Much of the evidence, even with the deed, is circumstantial, but the state insurance board has agreed to hear the case. Peter is to appear before them in September to present his company's testimony. The company's work is expanding, and that means the insurance company needs representation here in this area. They have appointed Peter to the newly established job as the Michigan regional manager of affairs. They want him to set up his office right here in Muskegon and be available to investigate other insurance concerns Chicago fire might have. What do you think of that, Alex?"

"Wow! This is great. I can't wait to tell Priscilla."

Just then their old friend Phillip appeared at the door. He opened it widely, and the ever-beautiful Priscilla appeared. She set aside all pretense of composure, rushed over to the astonished Alex, and threw her arms around his neck. "Isn't this all so exciting, Alex? I'm so happy about what the future holds for us..." Then, embarrassed, she stopped and settled herself as Addy and Phillip exchanged curious, though knowing glances.

"Yes, you both should know." Alex solemnly took Priscilla's hand, and standing proudly next to her, he explained, "I have asked Priscilla to consider becoming my wife." At that, his voice seemed to stumble, as if it was hard for him to get out the right words. "And she has said yes!" Then he added quickly, "I am by no means financially able to offer her support at this time. However, with Peter coming to Muskegon to set up his office, it does give us hope for the future once my employment is more secure."

Everyone beamed and looked ahead to a new, better day and a fulfilling, rewarding life in this ever-changing lumber town.

Chapter 17

Year 2000

Meg wanted to hear more about the picture, so she urged me on.

"Yes, it is a picture of a boy and a dog. Well, I'm not sure exactly. No, I don't mean it that way. I am very sure it is a picture of a young boy. It is a posed photographer's picture of a five-to- eight-year-old boy sitting in a chair. This is a sepia picture, so it's obviously old. It looks quite similar to other pictures I have seen from around the turn of the century, especially because of the old Victorian chair in which the boy is seated.

"Oh, my Lord. Not another mystery? What does this boy have to do with anything or with this house?"

"I have no idea yet about the boy. He will have to be researched at a later date. My point is that I didn't know the picture had any significance until you told me your story. It isn't the boy in the picture who is significant. It is the dog. It is also significant that I have kept this time-worn, hundred-year-old picture since I found it for no apparent reason, until now.

"Go on. You've got me hooked."

"Well, I had to look closely before I realized the problem. It is the dog that is out of place in the picture."

"How so?"

"Well, it is hard to explain, but I'll try. The picture of the dog is not a clear image like the one of the boy. The dog is a cloudy image, sort of out of focus. More intriguing yet, I think that part of the dog's image was sketched in and completed by hand."

"Now hold on. You're telling me you found a picture of a boy and a dog. Why do you think my ghost dog is this dog? I don't get it. What is the connection?"

"You'll see when I go get the picture. The dog image does not seem to belong in the picture. I believe it showed up in the photographer's picture, so he tried to make it look real by sketching in the details. You can especially see that most of the face and the paws were drawn in."

"OK, big thinker, where are you going with all this? Be quick, I'm dying of curiosity."

"I will keep the story short. I believe the dog was left here at the house when the owner moved out before the fire. He must have died in the fire. I don't believe it was planned for the dog to die in the blaze. Remember the conspirators had not planned to burn any houses that day, only the mill. The furniture had not been moved because of the planned fire but because the owner was in a hurry to get to Chicago. He'd packed that up prior to his departure."

"But why the haunting? Maybe I need to read up more on ghosts."

"Actually, I've been doing some research along those very lines myself recently. I believe the dog's spirit is still guarding this house like the real dog did originally. His master left him at the house as security when they removed the furniture. Who knows? Maybe Mr. Wallace had left some stuff to pick up later, including the dog. At any rate, the dog's job was not done, so he stayed on keeping watch in Mr. Wallace's house."

"He guarded it even when it was rebuilt?"

"Yes, he was guarding it when I first came, and he was still guarding it even after you moved it to this location."

"But the dog, he or she, has left now, hasn't it? Or do you believe it is still here guarding?"

"No, I now believe the dog's spirit has been released to go away but not because of any blessing or exorcism. In all my study and reading, I have found a large body of information about spirits staying around because they have some unfinished business or they have not been given permission to leave. I believe the spirit has now left because we figured out what happened here and told the story—the dog's story. That is, we finished his job. Now he can be released."

"Wow! I sure am glad I've been sitting down! I am dumb-founded. I certainly do have an amazing house here!"

"That you definitely do! Your house is special in many ways, and you've made it even more so by adding your creative touches. I see you have decided to restore the side and front porches and make them into one large porch. It will look great; a vast improvement over the two little rotted things that were falling off when you started this project. Also, the rear will be similar to the original, now that you've expanded the kitchen. That idea parallels the summer kitchen/rear porch concept of olden times. The idea remains the same—finding a cooler place in the heat of summer. Will you be moving your stove out there in summer too?"

"I seriously doubt that. Did you see how big that thing is! Also, the top of the extended kitchen room will be roofed and decked again for use in the summer. I doubt if we will screen it in, but maybe sometime in the future."

"Again, very similar to the original use," I added.

We both paused in our conversation, reviewing in our minds all of the changes, all of the discoveries, and all of the theories we'd envisioned about the origins and uses of the house.

Finally, I commented, "Thank you for sharing your new/old house with me. It is such a treasure."

Meg smiled, still a bit amazed by the latest developments about her house. "I promise I will do more research and be sure my restoration is as realistic and historically accurate as possible."

"We'll never know exactly the story of this house. I'd like Muskegon to collect more architectural archives. Some cities have whole libraries of pictures showing each house in the city over time. Some even detail in architectural drawings and pictures, the various stages and additions the houses have gone through. Manistee has done a tremendous job in that area. We have some pictures in the Muskegon Museum Archives but not nearly enough. I have a friend who works with those records. I'll ask him to dig into them for us to see if he can uncover any further information about your home."

"Thank you for sharing your insight and your imagination."

"Thank you for loving this old house and saving it. Who knows? Maybe we'll write a book about it someday."

Chapter 18

Year 1891

The Muskegon newspaper office was excited when it received a special delivery news release from Chicago. The editors were glad to reprint it for it had so much to do with settling much of the to-do left from the fire back in May. The release read:

"News article reprinted from the Illinois Legal Business News

Volume XCI, Date: October 14, 1891

STATE INSURANCE BOARD AWARDS SETTLEMENT

News was just released from the hearing room of the Illinois Insurance Board of Appeals in the case of the Chicago Fire Insurance Company vs. Smithson and Wallace Lumber and Saw Mills formerly of Muskegon, Michigan. Although the criminal courts have been unable to formulate hard enough evidence to prosecute the owners for any crime, the civil suit brought by the Chicago Fire Insurance Company has been decided in their favor. In an unusual turn of circumstances, the Chicago Fire Insurance Company has intern awarded the undisclosed settlement to one Ms. Addy Driscoll of Muskegon, Michigan, along with all other remaining assets of the said lumber mill operation. Under Ms. Driscoll's guidance, a foundation has been set up to help those who suffered losses in the fire. The appeal was presented ably by the Chicago Fire's West Michigan Regional Affairs Manager, Mr. Pretonius Frisk, who was quoted outside the hearing room as saying, "This is a fine day for justice. Justice has been awarded to the many folks who were hurt and whose property was destroyed by the lawless and greedy acts of self-serving rich men and their equally greedy organizations. Muskegon will be rebuilt both physically and spiritually with the generosity of this award."

Thanksgiving Day, 1891

"I propose a toast!" Peter rose and reached for his glass. Everyone around the table stopped their buzzing conversation and gave him their attention. Peter stood tall beside the ever-radiant hostess, Addy. Alex sat opposite them at the table heaped with a bountiful Thanksgiving feast. Priscilla's cousin, Maria, stopped scurrying from the kitchen as he spoke. Today, Priscilla was a guest at the table beside Alex. Maria was serving. Next to Priscilla sat Phillip, tall and with a ruddy complexion from his months of hard work with Geordie's teams. Across from Phillip sat Father Patrick from St. Mary's Parish.

"Today we have much to be thankful for. We need to pause to remind ourselves of that. Thank you, Father Patrick, for opening our meal with your prayer. We continue our Thanksgiving as we are reminded of the trying events that have occurred this past year." Peter paused before going on. "First, I propose a toast to our wonderful and gracious hostess, Miss Addy."

"Hear, hear!" all responded, and the clink of glasses resounded around the happy room.

Peter raised his glass again. "Also, I suggest we toast her generous offer to found the Muskegon

Benevolent Society with the settlement money she was awarded to help those families and businesses who have suffered damage or loss in our recent, tragic fire."

"Hear! Hear!"

"As the first act in her new organization, Addy has asked me to announce its first award." Pulling an envelope from his pocket, he handed it over to Priscilla. "Priscilla, will you open it please?" he instructed.

She sat down her glass and nervously broke the wax seal. She opened the envelope and pulled out a four-fold legal-size sheet of paper. "But what?" she stammered as her eyes quickly scanned the large page.

"It is a deed," Alex exclaimed as he leaned over and read it across her arm.

At this point, Addy spoke up. "My dear friend, the paper is the deed to the Pine Street property of Mr. and Mrs. Wallace. It is yours now. Also in that envelope is a grant for enough money to rebuild any house you want on that site."

Alex and Priscilla exchanged glances. "Oh, Miss Addy, might I rebuild the house as it was before? As you know, it was my only home, and I loved that house. It would be my dream to have it as my own. Alex and I hoped that one day we might be able to have a house of our own but never a house like that house. Oh, Miss Addy, you are so beyond generous. I cannot thank you enough." She dabbed at her tearing eyes with her napkin.

"The thanks are mine, my dear. We would not be enjoying this wonderful meal in this gracious dining room if not for your tireless work of rebuilding my own assets and turning this house into a home again."

"Ahem," Peter cleared his throat to get everyone's attention again before the two women started crying uncontrollably. "I have one more toast, if I may." Turning to Addy, Peter seemed to get flustered and stammered a little. Then, taking Addy's hand, he reached over and said, "A toast to our new life together. The beautiful Miss Driscoll has agreed to become my bride, Mrs. Petronius Frisk."

"Oh, yes! Hear! Hear!" everybody cheered, and Peter bent over gently, kissing her blushing cheek.

"And now that my office has officially moved to Muskegon, we can begin with a new Chicago

Connection and rebuild all of our lives anew right here together."

"Hear! Hear!" The clink of glasses and peals of laughter of beloved friends rang through the home, replacing the whispers of business treachery and greed. The house was alive again; it breathed the fragrance of renewal and growth. The entire group present gave thanks for their multitude of blessings; it was a true Thanksgiving.

Epilogue

I suppose it happens to all writers when a project gets its final period. One sits back and says, "C'est fini---it is done." Yet you no sooner say that and you continue to come up with more questions. As I have shared earlier, this was an unusual writing because the historical story actually wrote itself. You may have heard others say that about their writing, but I had never experienced it, so I still doubt it was possible. But I do know what happened. I am sure the story was there the entire time, just waiting for someone to write it.

I actually rewrote this whole story one time. I titled the new version *The Story House* because that was the only way I could describe it. The house was there and it held a story. I talked to the new owner about that second draft, and we decided the original version you see printed here was the best version. There was such an amazing connection between the

1891 story and that of today. I hope you have enjoyed our efforts to combine both stories. The owner and I have been true in reporting the events as they happened, mostly, giving the writer some poetic license to make the story move along.

Now I sit here drinking a cup of coffee, pleased with the product and smiling slightly. I'm pleased, I guess, but still I wonder. I wonder if the story is really done. Is it really over?

This story was inspired by and goes together with another historical fiction novel, *The Sawdust Fire* by Tom Carlson. I am bold enough to consider *From the Ashes* as a companion piece—a volume 2, if you will. We have conferred, and he too is not sure if the story is resolved yet. Maybe there is more to be said. We have simply brought up the idea. We have filled in some blanks and left others open. Maybe there is more information to uncover. I still have files of notes from my research as, I am sure, does Tom.

Many questions do arise. Whatever happened to the original participants? Did they fit into the transition and continuing development of Muskegon's industry? Maybe these books were not as much historical fiction as was originally thought. We have searched the local newspaper archives, but maybe we missed something. Maybe we should go back to research some more.

Hold it! What am I doing? I have just struggled for months to get this story ready for print, and I am off on another. Yet there seems to be something pulling my thoughts, drawing me on to another search. If there is no discovery, so be it. Would that prove the story goes no further? I don't think so.

And what if it does go on? Will you go on another adventure with me?

Acknowledgments

Tom Carlson can be contacted at:
tomnkayc@frontier.com.

Tom's book, *The Sawdust Fire*, is out of print, but copies are available from Tom or Ron.

R. C. (Ron) Robotham can be contacted through:
info@robowrites.com or
rcrobotham@msn.com.

Ron's website is: www.robowrites.com.

Much information is locally available about our Lumber Era and its activities and personalities. Much of that info can be found at Hackley Library and the Muskegon County Museum. Visits to two restored

Lumber Era homes are worth the effort, being full of artifacts that will give any visitor a sense of wonderment for the life and times of the previous century.

In Sight of Freedom

--An Old Forgotten Trail

Look for Robotham's third historical Fiction adventure –

COMING

JANUARY OF

2015!!

Join the Great Lakes captain, Jacques Bateau, as he travels the coastal towns of West Michigan transporting a mysterious cargo. The cargo has already traveled a dangerous journey from the south; now travelling on north, aboard the SS L'Etoile Polaire, they are always "In Sight of Freedom". Moving between the danger of slave catcher's guns and the caring arms of supporters, such as Jonathan Walker, the cargo travels to new life in a new land.

Made in the USA
Middletown, DE
02 June 2015